DAVENPORT HOUSE 5

DAVENPORT HOUSE 5

MARIE SILK

Davenport House Books by Marie Silk

BOOK ONE
Davenport House

BOOK TWO
Davenport House
A New Chapter

BOOK THREE
Davenport House
A Mother's Love

BOOK FOUR
Davenport House
Heiress Interrupted

BOOK FIVE
Davenport House
For the Cause

BOOK SIX
Davenport House
House Secrets

More titles coming in 2017:

Davenport House
Hard Times

Chapter I

Spring of 1917, Smith Manor House, Philadelphia

"Breakfast for you, Miss Abigail," Bridget announced as she entered the bedroom.

"Please leave it on the tea table for now," Abigail replied to her maid. She was in the room with her husband, Ethan, and seemed to be in the middle of a conversation.

Bridget left the room after setting the tray down and Ethan resumed his question to Abigail. "Are you certain about this?"

Abigail nodded. "It does not make sense to have this big house for only the two of us. I've enjoyed living here the past two years, but I thought—well I hoped—by now—" she stammered.

Ethan put his arms around her. "I know, I hoped so too. It will happen again when it's meant to. Perhaps we'll fill Davenport House with children and Clara will have second thoughts about asking us to stay with her."

Abigail forced a smile. "It will be lovely to see everyone at the house again. I only hope the new tenants here are kind to the servants. I plan to take Bridget with me when we move in with Mary and Clara."

"Have you told her yet?"

"No, but I believe that she will be very happy when I do tell her."

Just outside the manor house, Bridget was waiting anxiously near the front steps. She turned to glance at her reflection in the windows and smoothed her hair and dress for the third time. She wondered what could be taking so long. Then she felt her heart flutter when she could see a young man riding a bicycle toward the manor house. "Lawrence," she called when he came near. "I was worried there would be nothing in the post today."

"Well, there isn't anything," Lawrence chuckled. "I just wanted to see you. Do you have a minute?"

Bridget's eyes darted to the servants' entrance before she answered. "My Mistress has called a meeting with the staff and I will be late if I linger for too long."

"Then I'll be quick," he told her. "I brought something for you."

"You did?" Bridget grinned in anticipation.

Lawrence laughed. "I only hope it hasn't melted." He reached into his pocket and handed her a small square wrapped in foil. "It is from the Hershey Chocolate Company."

Bridget gasped. "Chocolate? Oh, how wonderful!"

"Aren't you going to try it?" he asked.

Bridget unwrapped the morsel for a small taste. "I would do anything to have chocolate every day," she sighed.

"If you were my girl, you would have chocolate every day," Lawrence assured her.

Bridget felt her cheeks burning. "Do you—want me to be your girl?"

Lawrence winked at her. "I'd better get the rest of these letters delivered. See you tomorrow?"

Bridget nodded. "I will be out at this time to collect the post." She turned to leave for the servants' entrance after watching Lawrence ride away on his bicycle. She finished the last of the chocolate and checked her reflection once more to ensure she looked presentable.

In the servants' lobby, the staff was just beginning to disperse after Abigail's announcement. "Mrs. Davis," Abigail discreetly addressed the housekeeper. "Where is Bridget?"

"I'm sorry, Madam. I told her of the meeting today. She—she had gone to collect the post—from that young man," she answered, giving Abigail a knowing look. "I will fetch her at once."

Abigail giggled. "Please, let her come in when she is ready. I'm afraid she might not have many more chances to—collect the post—after today."

"Yes, Madam," Mrs. Davis replied.

When Bridget entered the servants' lobby, she cringed in guilt when she saw that Abigail was already leaving.

"You are late," Mrs. Davis scolded her.

"I'm terribly sorry," Bridget apologized. "I was collecting the post."

Mrs. Davis raised her eyebrow. "Then where is it?"

Bridget looked down. "There was none today."

"I see. Then you should be returning to your duties, shouldn't you? You must make a good impression with the new tenants if you intend to keep your job."

"Yes, Mrs. Davis," Bridget replied. Then she looked up, confused. "What new tenants?"

Mrs Davis shook her head. "You were late for the news.

Mr. and Mrs. Smith are moving back to Davenport House in York County. New tenants arrive to this house next week. We will have a new Master and Mistress."

Bridget's eyes grew wide with uncertainty. "But who are the new tenants?"

Mrs. Davis shrugged. "We'll find out next week, I expect. But enough dawdling. You should report to the Mistress at once and apologize for missing her announcement. I imagine she wants you to begin packing her things."

Bridget swallowed her anxiety and went up the servants' stairs to Abigail's bedroom. "Come in, Bridget," Abigail said cheerfully when she saw her at the door.

"Miss Abigail, I'm sorry I missed your announcement to the staff," she apologized.

"It's alright," Abigail answered kindly. "I was going to speak to you in private anyway. You see, we have decided to move back to Davenport House. My brother Sam is there…and of course my sister Mary is there as well. We can no longer justify the expense of living here. We intend to let out the manor house and compensate Clara for our accommodations with her. It will benefit all of us to make this transition."

Bridget nodded in understanding, but did not ask the many questions that were making her head spin. She had come to work at the manor house to be Abigail's maid, and now worried what the new Master and Mistress might be like.

Abigail noticed the concern in Bridget's face and quickly continued, "I wonder if you would like to come with me. Mrs. Davis seems to think you have reason to want to stay here…"

Bridget could feel her cheeks burning red. "I don't

know why Mrs. Davis would say that," she replied quickly. "I want to go wherever you go, if you will have me."

Abigail smiled. "I have enjoyed your company these past years and I'm afraid I would miss you too much if you did not come with me. I telephoned Clara about it this morning and she explained that her servants' quarters are full and she has more than enough maids."

"Oh," Bridget said suddenly. "I'm sure Fiona won't mind if I share a room with her. I won't get in anyone's way."

"I'm certain your sister will be glad to see you again," replied Abigail. "But after discussing it with Clara, it is clear that an additional maid in her house would be redundant. It is why I want to ask you to come with me as my companion."

Bridget held her breath, wondering if she could be hearing right. Her heart pounded in her ears.

"Well, would you?" Abigail prodded.

"Oh! Yes, of course! I just—I can't believe it!"

"Wonderful," Abigail responded. "Now let us begin preparing for the move."

On the day of the move, Bridget waited anxiously for the post to arrive. She had not seen Lawrence since the day that Abigail announced the move. Bridget smiled when she could finally see him approaching on his bicycle. "Lawrence," she greeted with a smile. "I have some news."

"And I have some more chocolate for you. Sorry I have not been able to see you the last days. My mother is ill again and I had to care for her."

Bridget frowned in concern. "Oh, I am sorry about your mother. Will she be alright?"

Lawrence nodded. "Now, what is this news you have?"

"I am moving back to Davenport House in York

County. It's where I first began to work as a maid. My sister Fiona is the housekeeper there."

Lawrence looked downcast. "You're…leaving?"

"I'm terribly sorry. I don't wish to leave you, of course, but I am lucky to be gaining a new position. My Mistress has asked me to be her own companion."

"Is that why you're dressed fancy today?" he asked.

Bridget nodded with a smile. "The Mistress of Davenport House has enough maids already. She is a very rich lady who never married." Then Bridget said in a whisper, "Miss Clara is a suffragette, you see."

Lawrence raised his eyebrows. "Oh, I see."

"Will you come visit me at Davenport House? I will have more freedom as a lady's companion than I had as a maid."

Lawrence sighed thoughtfully. "I was offered a job in Yorktown not long ago. I turned it down because I wanted to be near you."

Bridget's heartbeat quickened at his words. "You turned down a job so you could be near me? Now I feel guilty for accepting this new position. Perhaps it's not too late to tell Miss Abigail that I've changed my mind, and will stay here."

"No, don't do that," Lawrence said. "I will talk to my boss and take that job in Yorktown."

"You will?" she gasped in delight. "And you will come see me at the house?"

"I will come see you at the house," Lawrence grinned. He took Bridget's hand and moved it to his lips, softly kissing it all over.

Bridget giggled in embarrassment. "Lawrence, what if someone sees?"

He looked at her mischievously, then pulled a stack of

letters and a square of chocolate from his messenger bag. "All anyone will see is a man who is in love with a beautiful girl. Here is the post for the house today, *Miss* Bridget. But the chocolate is only for you," he said with a wink. "I look forward to seeing you soon at Davenport House."

Later that evening, Abigail and Ethan were received warmly by Ethan's sister, Mary. Mary and her husband, Dr. Hamilton, also lived in the house with Clara Davenport, who was Mistress of the house.

"My dear brother!" Mary cried as she threw her arms around Ethan. She laughed when he briefly lifted her off the ground.

"Did you miss us?" he asked her.

"Terribly!" Mary replied. "I'm delighted that we will all be together again."

"Where are the others?" asked Abigail.

"Clara had a meeting at the town hall, and William is still at the clinic. I am the only one home tonight." Mary turned to greet Bridget, who stood awkwardly behind Abigail. "I nearly did not recognize you, Bridget. Welcome back to Davenport House."

"Thank you, Mrs. Hamilton," she replied shyly.

"You must call me Mary now," she insisted. Bridget nodded in response. "I imagine you are tired from your journey. The maids will take your things and get you settled in. Let us have tea in the sitting room in the meantime."

"Sounds lovely, Mary. Thank you," Abigail replied. She and Ethan followed Mary to the sitting room while Bridget stayed behind, hoping to see her sister.

"Fiona!" Bridget whispered happily when she saw her in the Hall.

"My dear little sister!" Fiona cried back. "You look fabulous—like a proper lady!"

Bridget giggled. "Can you believe it? Abigail gave me this dress just yesterday. Boy, it is strange to call the family by their given names. I will never be used to it."

"Of course you will get used to it, and I am happy for you," Fiona told her sincerely. "You'll also love the room I've prepared for you upstairs. It used to be Mrs. Price's room. I remember you saying it was your favorite."

"How wonderful! I'm afraid that any moment, I might wake up from this dream and be a housemaid downstairs again!"

Fiona laughed. "Heaven forbid. Mother and Father have been so proud since they heard of your promotion. It's all they could write about in their letters to me."

"I do have other news," Bridget said quietly. "Come to my room after tea and I will tell you all about him."

" 'Him'?" Fiona giggled. "Now I am dying to know." Bridget smiled in a teasing way before heading to the sitting room for tea.

When the others had retired to bed, Fiona went to Bridget's new upstairs bedroom. "Come sit on this marvelous bed with me," Bridget insisted.

Fiona flopped onto the bed and sighed happily. "You are lucky. I would give anything to sleep like this every night. Now, you must tell me everything. Do you have a beau?"

Bridget looked dreamily at the ceiling. "His name is Lawrence. He is Irish, of course. I wouldn't dream of taking a man who was not to meet Father."

Fiona sat up straight. "Is it as serious as all that?"

Bridget gave her a solemn look. "I think he will ask me

to marry him. Lawrence has already said that he is in love with me."

Fiona's eyes were wide. "Goodness! You will be engaged for at least two years, then."

Bridget shrugged. "Not if Father allows me to be married now. As long as I have his permission, the court will let me marry before I'm eighteen."

Fiona put her hand over her heart. "I can't imagine you married now. You must give me a moment to let this news sink in."

Bridget put her hand on her sister's shoulder. "Lawrence has promised to come see me here at the house. I know that when you meet him, you will approve of him at once. Then, you can write to Father about how much you approve so it is not so difficult when the time comes to ask him." Fiona and Bridget giggled together and continued talking into the night.

The next morning, Clara cheerfully greeted Abigail, Ethan, and Bridget at the breakfast table. "I am glad to see you all looking so well."

"We missed you at tea last night. Do the meetings really run so late?" Abigail asked.

Clara nodded. "They must if we are ever to get the vote. There are women staging demonstrations in Washington as we speak. It is important to be heard, and to be heard, we must first be organized."

"I admire all the work you have put in, Clara," Mary remarked, then looked around the room. "I don't know why William has not come to breakfast yet. He is usually the first one here, but I suppose he had a late night at the clinic."

William walked into the dining room just then with a grave expression. He held a newspaper in his arm. He glanced at the breakfast buffet, but instead of approaching it, he sat down at the table with the newspaper. "I'm afraid there is bad news," he said in a low voice. He handed the paper to Mary and Ethan who sat across from him. Mary gasped when she read the headline.

"What is it?" Clara asked. Abigail and Bridget looked at the others in suspense.

William answered mournfully. "America has declared war on Germany." The table went silent for several minutes.

"What is going to happen now?" Bridget asked timidly.

"Our military is recruiting more men to be sent to fight with the English and French. But if they cannot find enough men to volunteer," William said, looking toward Ethan, "it will no longer be by choice that we are sent to fight."

Chapter 2

Summer of 1917, Davenport House

"Ethan?" William called into the stable, approaching with a the latest newspaper. "There's something you should see."

Ethan was tending to the horses when William walked in. "More news of the War?" he asked.

"I'm afraid so," William answered, handing him the paper.

Ethan read the words on the page and nodded. "I guess we all knew it was coming. Abigail won't like this at all."

"I can't say I blame her," replied William.

"I could ask for an exemption. Perhaps they won't call me to fight," Ethan thought aloud.

Samuel, the young man who managed the grounds at Davenport estate, walked into the stable just then. "What's going on?" he asked when he saw Dr. Hamilton.

Ethan shook his head and held the paper out to him. "Here, you can see it for yourself."

Sam held up his hand. "That's alright, you can just tell me."

"It's a new law that requires men to sign up for military

service," William explained. "Every man age twenty-one to thirty."

Sam grimaced. "Does that include you, Dr. Hamilton?"

William chuckled. "I am German. They wouldn't want me anyway. But if they did, I am too old for their Draft. At least while the cutoff is still thirty…"

"You're too old and Sam's too young. But—I'm twenty-two. I guess I'll go down to the war office and see if there's a way I can get out of it."

"I would never help those English," Sam remarked, beginning to get angry. "Especially not after what they did to us in Dublin last year."

Ethan looked at him sadly. "Abigail told me about it. It was a terrible thing to happen to your relatives."

"What will you do about this Draft?" William asked.

Ethan shrugged. "I'll go to the war office and say I can't help them."

In the drawing room of Davenport House, Fiona stepped in to address Clara. "Mr. Valenti is waiting outside for you, Miss Clara."

"He is?" she asked in surprise. "I don't remember ordering the car."

"He has just walked over from next door. I think he only wants to talk to you," Fiona replied.

Clara left the room to meet her neighbor and chauffeur, Phillip Valenti, on the outside steps the house. "Good afternoon," she greeted. "Have you come to see me?"

"I signed up for service at the war office today. They'll give me papers if I help them with this War, so I'll be leaving for training soon. I thought I should offer to give Sam driving lessons in the meantime. That way, you'll have someone to take you to town when I'm away."

"I've been so busy that I suppose I forgot about all this happening with the War. When will you have to go?" Clara asked with a hint of concern in her voice.

"Next week is when I go to training camp," he answered. "I have enough time to teach Sam about the car, and my sister Serena will watch the children while I'm gone." Phillip smiled. "But when I come back, I'll be a real American."

Clara managed a smile too. "I'm happy for you, Phillip. And I would be grateful if you could teach Sam to drive before you leave. Thank you."

Phillip nodded. "Of course. It's been a pleasure working for you, Clara."

After Phillip spoke with Clara, he drove Abigail and Bridget into town for shopping. They passed the local war office which was set up next to the general store. "I've never seen such a line at the war office before," remarked Abigail. "I wonder why so many are enlisting today." Bridget appeared to be daydreaming and did not answer. Abigail giggled and asked, "Have you heard from your young man?"

Bridget snapped out of her trance and felt her cheeks burning. "I have not heard from him. He promised to come visit me at the house, but he must be held up in Philadelphia."

"Do you suppose he enlisted?" Abigail questioned.

"I should hope not! He wouldn't have done so without telling me. He is probably on his way to see me now. I'm certain he will come…" Bridget trailed off.

Abigail smiled at her. "I'm certain he will."

Later that evening when Abigail was dressing for dinner at the house, Ethan entered the bedroom sorrowfully.

"Where have you been all day?" she asked when he came into the room. She then noticed he appeared downcast. "What has happened?" she asked quickly.

"I have bad news," he started. "I went to the war office today…"

"You did? We must have just missed you. Bridget and I saw a long line of men standing outside. Why did you go?"

"There's a new law. That's why you saw it like that today. Every man over twenty-one and under thirty who doesn't sign up for service will be punished."

Abigail looked at him in dismay. "Ethan, trust me, you want nothing to do with those people. Not with this War. They can't make you fight against your will."

"That's just it—they can. I went to find out if there was an exception for me, but the military won't allow it." He paused with a labored sigh. "They want me to start training next week."

Abigail gasped. "Ethan, tell me you won't really go! My cousins were not even part of that Rebellion in Dublin, and the English murdered them all! You cannot join such people!"

Ethan held up his hands in defeat. "I don't have a choice. Would you rather me be in jail for refusing?"

Abigail felt tears stinging her eyes. "This can't be happening." She wiped her face and lowered herself onto the bed. "We can go to California to be with your pa. We can go to Canada. Anything but this!"

Ethan kneeled on the floor in front of her. "I'm sorry, Abigail. I can't run away like a criminal. The lieutenant in Yorktown said the War is almost over anyway. All we have to do is go help the French finish things up, and we'll be back home before you know it."

Abigail lay back on the bed. "I don't want to go to

dinner tonight. Not until we find a solution that does not involve your going to France." They stayed in the room for the rest of the night, but their talks never came to a solution.

The house was grim the day of Ethan's departure for training camp. Abigail was inconsolable and the others could hear her weeping in the bedroom. "Don't do this, I beg of you," she cried.

"I have to post this letter to Pa," Ethan said in a low voice while he sealed an envelope.

"It's not too late," Abigail persisted. "We can get on the next train for California and they will never find you."

Ethan stood up from the writing desk and gazed sorrowfully at Abigail on the bed. "I have to leave now," he said gently.

Abigail cried into her hands and did not look up at him. She soon felt his arms holding her tight and the warmth of him whispering in her ear, "I'll be back as soon as I can. I love you more than anything." That feeling of warmth soon vanished when she heard his footsteps toward the door, then the door open and close. Abigail looked up from her hands. Ethan was gone.

William and Mary waited at the bottom of the staircase. Clara also stood nearby. Ethan walked down the stairs slowly, hanging his head. "Abigail won't come down," he mumbled.

Mary hugged him tightly but could feel her heart sinking into her stomach when she realized that her brother was really leaving. "I'll take care of Abigail as best I can. I promise," she said to him.

"Thank you, Mary," he replied emotionally.

"Are you ready?" William asked him.

Ethan nodded and followed William to the car in the front drive. He looked back at the house behind him, hoping to catch a glimpse of Abigail in the bedroom window. She was not there. She was racing down the staircase after drying her face, hoping to say a proper goodbye to him, but the car had already left. "Am I too late?" she asked breathlessly.

"They have just gone," Mary said gently.

"Oh Mary, I never told him goodbye, or even that I loved him. What if it takes months or years for him to return?"

Mary put her arms around Abigail. "He knows you love him. Don't worry about that."

Clara gave her a compassionate look. "Is there anything I may do to help you feel better today?"

"Thank you, Clara, but I don't see how I can feel better until we are all together again, as it should be." She slowly returned up the stairs to her room.

"Do you think she'll be alright?" Clara asked Mary.

"Give her time," Mary responded. "I believe we will see her recover if she finds a worthy cause to keep her occupied."

"But Abigail doesn't believe in this War," Clara said.

"No, she does not," sighed Mary. "Clara, we should not forget about Serena Valenti. I understand that Phillip has also left today for training camp."

Clara nodded sadly. "He did tell me that he was leaving. Oh Mary, I do hope the men will be alright."

"We must believe that they will. Otherwise, we will be miserable until their return. For now, let us be sure to support poor Serena. She is at the farmhouse alone with the children and she needs to know we will be here for her if there is anything she needs."

"Good idea, Mary," Clara agreed. "Should we walk over now to talk to her?"

Mary hesitated. "I think I should go to Abigail now."

"Then I will go to the farmhouse and pay Serena a visit," decided Clara. Mary went up the staircase to be with Abigail, and Clara left for the Valentis' farmhouse.

In the servants' quarters of the house, Bridget was waiting in Fiona's bedroom. "Bridget? What are you doing down here?" Fiona asked curiously.

Bridget looked up with her tear-stained face. "Abigail wishes to be alone. She is terribly grieved that her husband has left today."

"Poor Miss Abigail," Fiona answered.

"Fiona, do you think that Lawrence would have joined the army without telling me? It has been months and I have still not heard from him."

"Did you write to him?"

"I would have if only I knew his address. I sometimes wonder if I should return to the manor house just to see if he is alright. He should have written or come to visit me by now."

"If he loves you, then he will come," Fiona assured her.

Bridget smiled. "I'm certain that he loves me. I can't wait for you to meet him, Fiona. I hope that Lawrence and I are married by summer's end!"

"You will surely be married before I am," laughed Fiona. "I will be a housekeeper into my old age."

"You'll find someone, just as I have," Bridget encouraged. "Don't give up hope just yet."

At the Valentis' farmhouse, Clara was about to knock on the door. She could hear the children inside the house, asking questions about their father. "But when will Papa be back?" rang the voice of Gabriella, who was seven years old.

"He'll be back before we know it. Now, finish eating your breakfast so you can go play," Serena's voice answered. Clara knocked softly on the door. Serena timidly greeted her. "Miss Davenport, good morning."

"Good morning," answered Clara. "I understand that your brother has left for military service, and I wanted to tell you that you are welcome to come to us if you need anything. If you need a ride to town, Sam can take you in our car. And if you need help with the children, we are just a short walk away."

Serena put her hand to her heart and breathed in relief. "Thank you, Miss Davenport. I am grateful that you have come today. I don't know how long Phillip will be."

"Please do not hesitate if there is anything you need," she replied. "And please, call me Clara. I hope that we may become friends while the men are away."

"Thank you, Clara. It's not so easy to meet people who are generous to us. It's one of the reasons my brother volunteered for this War. He thinks people might be nicer to us, so long as he has his American papers. But you have been kind to us all along. I'll be sure to stop by if there is anything I need. Thank you again, Clara, and good day."

Clara left the farmhouse feeling content. When she returned to the house, she nearly walked into the drawing room, but stopped suddenly when she noticed a man sitting on the sofa. Clara quietly backed away from the entrance before the man could see her. She then whispered to Fiona, who had just come into the Hall. "Why is someone in the drawing room?"

"Mr. Blake has come to see you, Miss Clara," she answered. "I could not find you to announce his arrival."

"But, who is he?" asked Clara.

"He said he is our neighbor."

Clara again peered into the doorway of the drawing room, but this time the man looked her way and stood up quickly. " 'Afternoon, Ma'am," he greeted.

Clara suddenly felt nervous, but tried to remain calm as she went to meet him properly. "Good afternoon," she replied.

"My name's Joe Blake. I just bought the five hundred acres next to you and came to introduce myself. Is the lady of the house in?"

"I'm pleased to make your acquaintance, Mr. Blake. I am Clara Davenport."

Joe reacted in surprise. "Oh! You're the lady of the house? I expected someone different."

"How do you mean?"

"Well, I was told the Miss Davenport who lived here was an old spinster." Joe regretted his words instantly while Clara gaped in horror. "I meant to say—you're not an old spinster! I don't know why anyone would say that about you—" He quickly made his way for the exit. "I'm sorry, Ma'am, I have to go. I'm just next door if you need anything!" He bolted through the room and out the front door, leaving Clara bewildered in the drawing room.

Chapter 3

"Howdy, Neighbor," Joe Blake greeted Sam on the warm summer day. Sam was letting the horses out to the pasture when Joe arrived.

"Howdy," answered Sam. "How's the ranch going?"

"Well, could be better. That cotton-pickin' Draft stole both of my ranch hands. It's tough to find a man to work these days. I told the war office I couldn't handle it all on my own, but they said the boys were more needed in France. Now it's just me handling the ranch alone. I wondered if you might like some extra work. I can pay you well."

"Extra work!" laughed Sam. "Miss Davenport lost her driver and the stable hand to the military. Now I'm doing the job of three men."

Joe laughed too. "Then I guess I feel guilty asking you to lend a hand for a minute."

Sam looked toward the house. "I wish I could, but I gotta bring the car around for Miss Davenport."

Joe smiled wide. "I met Miss Davenport just last week. Boy, is she beautiful or what? How is that lady not married yet?"

Sam laughed. "I just work here. You could go ask her why."

Joe groaned. "I already made a fool of myself when I first visited. I just wondered why she's still unmarried, that's all. Anyway, if you ever find some extra time, my offer stands. I'll be happy to take any help I can get at the ranch."

"Thanks, but I'll be busy here for a while," Sam replied. "Besides, I can't let Miss Davenport down."

"No, I wouldn't want that either. See you, Sam."

At the town hall in Yorktown, Clara was concluding a meeting for the support of women's suffrage. "We've all worked hard to come this far, and I have some cheerful news for you all. I will be hosting a garden party at my estate next week and you are all invited." The ladies whispered excitedly amongst themselves. At the end of the meeting, several ladies rose from their seats to speak with Clara and express their anticipation of the garden party. Clara was surprised to see a new face among those in attendance; not surprised because the face was new, but because it belonged to a man. Clara noticed him right away when the meeting started and he seemed to be staring at her, even while the other ladies were giving their speeches.

Clara seated herself at a table to organize her notes while the others left the town hall. She looked up from her seat when one of the ladies approached with the stranger.

"Miss Davenport, here is Mr. Collins. He is new in town and expressed a desire to meet you," she explained.

"I'm pleased to meet you, Mr. Collins," Clara greeted cheerfully. "It's always refreshing to make the acquaintance a man who supports our cause."

Mr. Collins shrugged. "I don't know about that. I mostly came to see to see what your cause is all about."

"It's the simple request that women be recognized as equals in the voting populace," Clara answered.

Mr. Collins shrugged. "I don't see what difference it makes. A woman will simply vote for whoever her husband tells her to."

Clara raised her eyebrow at him and continued, "Does not a married woman deserve a voice of her own? And what if a woman has no husband?"

Mr. Collins laughed. "You got me there, Miss Davenport. You know, those posters going around town make you suffragettes look like crazy old women. You don't fit that description at all, Miss Davenport. In fact, I bet if more men could see what a real suffragette looks like, a lot more of them might come to your meetings. I know I'll be attending more often."

Clara was not sure if she should be flattered or offended, but she felt a little of both. She responded quickly after gathering the last of her notes, "Then I am sure to see you again. Good day, Mr. Collins." He smiled at her before he turned to leave the room. When Mr. Collins had gone out the door, Clara whispered to the lady who introduced him. "Isabel, what do you know about Mr. Collins?"

"This is the first I've seen him," Isabel replied with a wry smile. "But he certainly seems to know about you."

"How could he?" asked Clara.

"You are popular in town now. Many of the young people look up to you. Although, from the way Mr. Collins was staring at you, I think he is interested in more than only your politics."

"Oh, honestly Isabel!" Clara said, feeling a rush of redness to her cheeks. "I doubt very much that is why he came today."

Isabel smiled knowingly at Clara before she left the town hall. "I can't wait for your garden party, Clara."

Clara later returned to the house and stepped out back to wander in the gardens. She envisioned the party taking place in the clearing, and a delightful buffet set up near the rose bushes. She heard a sound coming from behind the bushes, like a hoofed animal was walking along the other side. Clara held her breath. She thought one of the horses must have wandered into the garden. When she peered from the other side of the bushes, she could see that the animal was not one of the horses. Clara gasped at the sight of a cow eating from the flower bed below. "Stop that at once! Shoo! Shoo!" she demanded. The cow did not shoo, but looked up at Clara with a disinterested expression before it went back to chewing on the flowers. Clara hurried to the stable in the hopes of finding Sam, but he was not there. She groaned as she held her skirt in her hand and tried to run to the new neighbor's cottage. She was flustered and out of breath when she got there and pounded on the door. "Mr. Blake! Mr. Blake!"

Joe answered in surprise. " 'Afternoon, Miss Davenport."

Clara tried to catch her breath. "Your cow—I saw it—in my garden!"

Joe chuckled. "That would be Ol' Bess. I wondered where she went." Joe peered around Clara. "Where is she?"

"Still eating my flower beds, I'm sure!" she cried.

"Oh. I thought you would've brought her with you."

Clara looked aghast. "I don't know how to bring a cow!"

Joe was unsuccessful at stifling his smile. "I'm sorry, Miss Davenport. I'll go get her right away." He put on his hat and ran straight to the gardens. Clara picked up her skirt again and went as quickly as she could, but Joe was already heading toward her with Ol' Bess before she reached the gardens. "I apologize, Ma'am. Looks like she got most of your flowers."

Clara put her hand to her forehead in despair. "But I am to have a garden party on Saturday."

"I'll replace them just as soon as I can. Promise," he told her, crossing his heart.

Clara sighed in defeat. "Fine. Just please see to it that your cow stays on your side of the fence."

Joe smiled wryly. "I'll do my best, Ma'am."

Later than evening, Mary was in her bedroom getting ready for dinner when William walked into the room unexpectedly. "You're home," Mary greeted happily. "I've missed you."

"Did you?" he smiled back at her. Then he asked carefully, "How is Abigail today?"

Mary frowned. "She is still taking meals in her room. Bridget stays with her all day now. I've asked her to ride the horses with me, but she is not interested. But I also fear that the more I see her, the more I will worry about Ethan, myself. I have been reading to keep my mind off of him."

William hugged her and kissed her hair. "It is a good idea. What have you been reading?"

Mary blushed suddenly and William wondered why she went silent. She finally answered, "Gray's Anatomy."

William laughed. "I had no idea it was interesting enough to read for pleasure."

"Well," Mary began shyly, "I was looking at the illustrations mostly." She went to the armoire and pulled the book out from under the linens, flipping to the page she wanted to show William.

He raised his eyebrows in surprise. "The human embryo," he read from the page.

"I'd like to know what to expect—when it happens for us—if it happens for us," Mary said quietly. "It seems all the ladies I know delivered a child within their first year of marriage. I had a telegram from Nellie today announcing her second child. I worry there must be something wrong with me."

"Mary, why didn't you tell me that you were worried about this?"

Mary turned her face away from him. "I didn't want to bother you about it, and I kept hoping that it would happen by now. But since it hasn't…maybe it won't."

He gently put his arms around her. "Do you know how many women come into the clinic every week with the same worries? Not everyone has a child right away, Mary. It's as if the little ones have a mind of their own when they are going to decide to come into the world."

"Do you ever tell the women to do things like wait for the full moon or take cinnamon with honey?" Mary asked curiously.

William chuckled. "Those are just wives' tales, Mary. I usually tell them to be patient. More often than not, they are back within a year or two with a child ready to be delivered."

Mary sighed. "You are fortunate to be there when the babies are born. I have no idea what to expect when the time comes."

William brushed her hair to the side. "I expect there will be more deliveries than I can handle when the Spring comes."

"What do you mean?"

"Well," he laughed. "It will be nine months after the Draft started."

Mary giggled. "I suppose I did not think about that."

"I have to think like that so I can make the necessary arrangements," William replied. Then he looked thoughtful for a moment. "Would you like to accompany me to a birth?"

Mary's face lit up instantly. "Could I? Do you think the family would mind?"

"I will talk to them beforehand. I don't know why I haven't thought of this before. You may come see what it is all about and perhaps even lend a helping hand. There are no midwives in Yorktown, and I need all the help I can get."

"There used to be a midwife," Mary told him. "She was run out of town on account of practicing witchcraft. Can you believe it?"

William looked surprised. "When was this?"

"Many years ago. I was told about it when I was a child, and it was a terrible ordeal from the sound of it. I suppose the women of the county have been too frightened to become the next midwife after what happened to the last. Her name was Greta Jenkins."

"Well, I sure wish she was still around. I could use the help. Now Mary, you should understand that sometimes deliveries take a lot of time, and they may happen any hour day or night. Are you certain you want to attend the next one?"

"Yes, I am certain I want to go with you!" She clasped her hands together in delight. "I'm so excited, I don't know how I will sleep tonight!"

In the dining room that evening, Mary, William, and Clara were the only ones seated at the table. "I hope Abigail starts dining with us again soon," Clara remarked. "How much longer do you suppose she'll keep to her room?"

"It's hard to say," Mary answered. "But I have thought of a plan to keep her occupied."

Clara seemed intrigued. "What is this plan of yours?"

"I thought I might suggest that she visit Serena. Perhaps she will find ways to help her and it can take both of their minds off the War."

"A good idea, Mary," Clara smiled. "And I have some happy news. I am hosting a garden party for the women's suffrage group next week. I think it's time we had a party to cheer us after all the hard work we have put in."

"Brilliant, Clara," Mary responded. "A garden party will be just the thing to help us feel merry again."

In the stable on Davenport Estate, Sam was bringing the horses in from the pasture and guiding them into their stalls. He was surprised to see that Fiona had walked in. "Hello," he greeted.

Fiona smiled shyly. "Hello. You received something in the post today. I was going to hand it to you at dinner but never saw you come in to eat."

"I was helping Joe at the ranch," Sam answered. "Thanks for bringing it to me."

Fiona nodded. "You're welcome. Have a good evening, Sam." She turned to leave.

"Fiona, just a moment…can you tell me how my sister is doing?"

Fiona turned around to face Sam. "She is still keeping to her room."

"I figured," Sam replied. He looked like he wanted to say more, but he remained quiet.

"Is there something else?" Fiona asked gently.

Sam looked embarrassed. "Uh—there is—something," he stuttered. "You see, usually my sister helps me when I get a letter, but I don't want to bother her. Would—would you mind?" Sam opened the envelope and held the letter out for Fiona.

"Oh," she answered. "Of course I don't mind." She unfolded the page and began to read the words to him.

Dearest Samuel,

I'm sorry that your brother-in-law has to leave with the military. Abby must be terribly sad, for I know that I would be if it was you who had to leave for the war. I miss you dearly. When will you return to see me? I long for the day when our house will be finished and we can finally be married.

Cordially,
Jenny

Fiona looked up at Sam and handed him the letter. "She sounds lovely."

"Jenny is a real nice girl. I've been saving up for land to build our homestead. I've almost got enough money now. If I keep helping Joe on the ranch, I might even have enough by next Christmas," he explained proudly.

"I'm happy for you, Sam. I did not realize you had a fiance."

"I asked her right before I took this job. She's been waiting for me and I've been workin' as hard as I can so I don't disappoint her. I'll wait for Abby to feel better before I ask for help writing back to Jenny."

"I'd be happy to write your reply, if you'd like," Fiona offered.

"Thanks, Fiona. But I know how busy you are keeping

that house in order. My sister says you're as good as the last housekeeper who worked there twenty years."

Fiona felt her cheeks turning pink. "That was kind of Miss Abigail to say. I should get back to the house now. Just remember that I would be glad to help if you need to write back." Fiona then left the stable so that Sam could return to his work with the horses. When Fiona returned to the servants' lobby, one of the housemaids was waiting for her.

"Miss Clara was just asking for you," Nora said. "I told her that you were in the stable with Sam."

"Good grief, Nora. You didn't have to put it like that. All you had to say was that I would be right up," Fiona replied.

Nora shrugged. "I didn't know it was supposed to be a secret."

"He received a letter in the post today and I took it to him. You needn't make any more of it than it is," Fiona called over her shoulder as she went up the servants' stairs. She found Clara in the drawing room, having tea with Mary. "You asked to see me, Miss Clara?"

"Oh, hello Fiona," Clara said distractedly. "We wondered if you saw who brought the flowers and chocolate that were left on the front steps." She gestured toward a large bouquet of roses and an elegant box wrapped in pink ribbon.

"I did not see anyone come to the house, Miss Clara. Did the flowers and chocolate perhaps come with a note?"

"Oh, there was a note with it alright," giggled Mary.

"Oh," Fiona said, confused why the ladies would have asked her.

Clara laughed and handed the note to Fiona. "Here,

see what you can make of it." Fiona glanced over the words curiously.

To Miss Clara Davenport,

Consider this a peace offering.

From Your Secret Admirer

"Are you sure you didn't see anyone come to the house? Did you hear a car come up the drive?" Clara prodded.

"I'm sorry, Miss," Fiona replied, embarrassed that it must have been delivered while she was in the stable.

Mary then said playfully to Clara, "I think you know who it is, you just don't want to tell me."

Clara was thoughtful. "Since none of us heard a car approaching, I wonder if it was our new neighbor, Mr. Blake."

"Does he need to make peace with you?" laughed Mary, referring to the note.

"One of his cows got into our gardens and ruined the flower beds," Clara recounted impatiently. "I had to run all the way to his cottage to tell him to come get his cow!"

Now Mary was laughing hard. "How funny, Clara! You must have made an impression on Mr. Blake. I hope you will invite him to the garden party."

Clara covered her red cheeks. "I had not thought of that. He might not admire me once he attends a party of mine with so many outspoken ladies."

"Perhaps he is a progressive," Mary offered. "Please invite him, Clara. I want to see what this Mr. Blake looks like."

"Oh fine, if it will make you happy, Mary." Clara

turned to Fiona. "Could you see to it that Mr. Blake receives an invitation?"

Fiona nodded. "I'll see to it, Miss."

The next day, Clara visited Abigail in her room to tell her about the garden party. "I'm certain your party will be lovely, Clara," responded Abigail. "But I think I will stay in my room. I don't wish to see other people right now. I'm sorry to be such a bore."

"You are fine," Clara smiled. "Abigail…I've been thinking lately about Serena Valenti. I've offered to help her with anything she needs, but I wonder if she has been too timid to ask. I thought I should invite her to the garden party. Her family is back in Pittsburgh, and I don't believe she has any friends here in York County, so she must be lonely. I wonder if she might like to socialize with us a bit more…if only there was someone who could care for the children so she could leave the house…"

"Oh," Abigail said quickly. "I would be happy to care for the children if Serena wishes to attend the party." She then smiled for the first time since Ethan had left. "They are such dear children, Clara. Please tell Serena that I would be glad to help."

Clara smiled back and hugged Abigail. "You are the sweetest. I will go to the farmhouse and talk to her now."

Before Clara called on Serena, she went to the gardens behind the house to assess the damage done by Mr. Blake's cow. She walked around the hedges to see the other side and let out a scream when she ran into a man kneeling on the ground.

Joe looked at Clara with a startled expression. "Howdy," he finally said.

Clara held her hand over her racing heart. "I'm sorry, Mr. Blake. I was not expecting anyone to be out here."

"Neither was I," Joe laughed, rising to his feet. "I was just planting these new flowers for you as best I could. How does it look?"

Clara did not hear what he said. She was noticing his tanned, defined features, and wondering if he would confess to sending the flowers and chocolate.

"Um—I can keep working on them if it's not to your liking," he said nervously.

Clara snapped out of her daydream. "Oh! I'm sorry. Yes, the flower beds—they look fine."

Joe sighed in relief. "Thank you, Miss Davenport. I suppose this is the first time you've seen me that I haven't messed something up. Sorry about all that business with Ol' Bess. I'm gettin' the fence fixed where she broke out. Anyway, I hope you have a good day." Joe gathered his garden tools and began to walk away.

"Wait! Mr. Blake!" Clara suddenly called.

He turned around to face her. "Yes Ma'am?"

"I just wondered—well I wanted to know if—" she stammered, "—if you were coming to my garden party on Saturday."

Joe laughed. "When your maid brought the invitation, I thought it must be a mistake. I thought it must have been for a different neighbor. But sure I'll be there, if you want me to."

"I thought since you are new in the county, you might like to meet some of the townspeople. Although there likely won't be other men in attendance."

"No, I suppose the men are scarce nowadays because of the War," Joe said.

Clara looked at him curiously. "Aren't you worried they may call you to fight?"

Joe shook his head. "They won't be calling me. The government doesn't want farmers going over and leaving no one to tend the land here. They already gave me an exemption."

"I see," Clara replied, looking into his eyes. "Then I am glad you will be staying."

Joe chuckled. "I'm glad I will be staying too. See you on Saturday, Miss Davenport."

The day of the garden party arrived. Everyone gathered behind the house in the clearing where tables and chairs had been placed that morning. Mary walked alongside Clara near the hedges. "Is that your Mr. Blake?" she asked, nodding in the direction of the only man in attendance, who was surrounded by the other ladies.

Clara smiled shyly and nodded. Mary raised her eyebrow and said, "He is quite good looking."

"Oh stop it, Mary. I don't want to be red-faced if he ever makes his way over here to talk to me."

"Has he said anything to you about the flowers and chocolate?" Mary questioned.

"If it was he who brought them, he has not given any indication of it."

"I'll go ask him, if you'd like. I'm dying of curiosity," Mary teased. "You really should go save him, Clara. It looks as if those ladies are going to smother him."

Clara began walking toward Joe and he gave her a look a relief. She heard him saying, "If you'll excuse me, Ladies, I must have a word with Miss Davenport now." The ladies dispersed to the tea table, giving Joe and Clara a chance to walk alone in the garden.

"The ladies from town…they are very…welcoming…" he said.

Clara giggled. "I'm sorry about that. I suppose they were happy to see a man who they might convince with our cause."

"I don't need any convincing," said Joe. "A woman is just as much a person as a man. Why shouldn't they vote?"

Clara could not contain her smile. "It is just what I think! Thank you for saying so. You would not believe how many men are opposed to such a simple thing."

"I'm sorry about that, Miss Davenport. I hope you ladies get your vote. Although, I told your friends I would not be able to attend the meetings in town. I can't leave the ranch for too long. In fact, I should be getting back now."

"Oh," Clara said, trying to hide her disappointment. "Thank you for coming today, Mr. Blake."

"I wish you'd call me Joe," he told her. "We'll be seeing a lot of each other for many years to come."

Clara looked at him in confusion. "How do you mean?"

"I mean because we're neighbors," Joe answered with a laugh. "I never understood being formal with the people you see almost every day."

"Oh, I see," Clara said nervously. "Um—Joe—did you happen to come by the house recently and leave something on the front steps?"

Joe shook his head. "I haven't left anything here."

Clara searched his face to determine if he was teasing, but he seemed sincere. "I do hope we see you more often—when you're not too busy," she said finally.

Joe smiled. "I'm sure you will."

"And Joe—" Clara told him. "I agree with you that we need not be so formal. Please, call me Clara."

After Joe left the party, Serena Valenti approached Clara. "Thank you for having me for the party today," she said. "You ladies have been kinder to me than anyone."

"I am pleased you could attend," Clara replied. "It is the perfect day for a garden party. We won't have many more days like this, with the Autumn coming soon. Are you feeling the chill in the air already?"

Serena thought that Clara must be referring to the heavy sweater that Serena wore. "I'm sorry, I suppose one isn't supposed to wear such things to a garden party."

"No need to be sorry," Clara smiled. "I hope you will come to more of my parties in the future. Abigail did seem cheerful this morning when she left to care for your brother's children, and poor Bridget was relieved to have the day off. Please do not forget my offer to help if there is ever anything you need."

Serena returned to the farmhouse where Abigail was playing a game with the two children, Gabriella and Donnie. "Is the party over already?" Abigail said with a smile.

Serena nodded. "I'm grateful to you for staying with the children."

"I am happy to do this anytime, Serena. Truly. Is it terribly cool outside?" Abigail questioned, noticing Serena's sweater.

"It is still warm," she answered. Serena looked like she could not wait to remove the sweater, and when she finally did, Abigail understood why she wore it to the party. The shoulders of Serena's dress were ripped at the seams. "I've not had time to mend it," she explained sheepishly.

Abigail stepped closer to her and inspected the seams. "The only trouble is, the material has become threadbare. Even if we mend it, it will not stay together for long."

Serena nodded. "At least the weather will soon be cool and I will have a better reason to wear my sweater."

Abigail smiled compassionately and changed the subject. "I hope you will allow me to care for the children more often. I'm always available at the house."

"I may have to take you up on the offer. Thank you, and I hope you enjoy the rest of your day."

When Abigail attended breakfast in the dining room the next day, Mary and Clara were pleased to see her looking cheerful. "Good morning," Mary said happily.

"Good morning, Mary."

"Do you have any plans for the day, Abigail?" asked Clara.

"Bridget and I are going into town. We have shopping to do." The two of them finished their breakfast and were soon on their way to town in the car with Sam driving.

"I am glad to see Abigail feeling better," remarked Mary. "She seems to have a plan for passing the time while Ethan is away."

"And how are you feeling about it all, Mary?" asked Clara.

Mary looked down at her empty plate. "I hope he comes home soon. It was difficult enough to be separated from him when we lived only hours away from each other. Now he is a world away. I only hope he is alright."

Later in the afternoon, there was a knock at the door of the Valentis' farmhouse. Serena was delighted to see that Abigail had come to visit. "Hello Abigail," she greeted.

Abigail could hardly contain her smile. "I found some things in town that I thought you might like." She walked into the house and began to lay out two white blouses and two colorful skirts. "They are the fashion now."

Serena was hesitant. "You shouldn't have spent your money on me. I don't deserve it."

"Of course you do. You have been good enough to come live with your brother and keep his house and care for his children," Abigail replied.

Serena hung her head. "I am sorry to contradict you, but you are mistaken if you believe that is our situation. It is not I who am doing my brother the favor, but he who is helping me. No one else in my family will speak to me."

"Why wouldn't they?" Abigail questioned, seating herself in one of the chairs.

Serena was not sure how to answer. She sat across from Abigail and began quietly, "Before I came to live with Phillip, I had a child."

Abigail raised her eyebrows in surprise. "Oh? I did not realize you were a mother."

Serena nodded. "Some friends of mine in Pittsburgh have been raising my daughter as their own. Phillip offered his home to me when no one else would take me. I think you should know the truth if you think I deserve these nice clothes."

Abigail did not seem bothered. "What is your daughter's name?"

A smile crossed Serena's lips. "Angelina."

"It is a lovely name," Abigail replied. "You must miss her very much."

Serena nodded. "Every day. But I know my friends are raising her better than I could have."

"I see," Abigail said thoughtfully. "I do hope you accept the new clothes, Serena. You deserve to have something lovely to wear, whether you believe it or not."

CHAPTER 4

Autumn of 1917, France

The bitter rain fell and the mud ran deep, causing time to stand still for the soldiers in the trenches. They were shivering that day, awaiting their next order, and pushing the thoughts of hopelessness and despair behind them. "Advance! Advance!" the lieutenant-general was shouting. The deafening roar of artillery shells coupled with the cries of men nearly drowned out the order altogether. Phillip Valenti stared in anguish at the barricade before him, knowing it was all that was left between their regiment and the enemy. Just as Phillip took the first step forward, he felt a hand forcibly grab his shoulder.

"Valenti!" Ethan yelled into his ear, even though their faces were only inches apart. Phillip turned his head to lock eyes with him while Ethan continued. "If anything happens to me, swear that you will care for Abigail and Mary!"

"I swear!" Phillip cried back. "And if anything happens to me, look after my family! Be a father to my children!"

"I swear!" shouted Ethan. They soberly shook hands before charging past the safety of the barricade, rapidly approaching the peril at the front line. Bullets were flying and men were dropping to the ground, causing the realization to those left standing—that it would take a miracle for any of the them to return home alive.

Phillip continued to charge forward as he was told. His boots were heavy with mud from the trenches, and the rain poured down mercilessly, making it hard to distinguish the allies from the enemy. Phillip scarcely noticed that his pant leg had become soaked in more than only rain. He soon felt a throbbing, blinding pain and looked down at his leg. Blood ran down his boots and into the mud. He felt short of breath and suddenly discovered that he was lying on his back. He made the sign of the cross and began praying for mercy that the end would be quick before the Germans could capture him. But he felt himself being dragged backward and sideways. He lost all sense of direction and was unsure if the arms that pulled him were doing so to safety or to his demise.

A sudden sensation of free falling several feet down before hitting the ground caused him to shake with fright. It felt like falling into a grave. But when he opened his eyes again, he was aware that he was back in the trenches he had just left from, and shrapnel was being pulled from his leg. He winced in pain.

"Smith! Get back out there!" barked the lieutenant-general.

"He needs a medic!" Ethan shouted back.

"Him and everyone else! Now get out there!"

Ethan looked into Phillip's open eyes. "Don't forget what you swore!" After Ethan spoke the words, everything went black, and Phillip drifted into the deepest sleep he had in months.

That same night at Davenport House, after everyone

had been asleep for hours, William gently shook Mary awake. "Mary, you need to get up."

She groggily looked around the dark room. "What it is? What's happening?"

William chuckled. "It's time. I just got the call from Mr. Daniels."

Mary gasped and sat upright in bed, suddenly feeling the pounding of her heart in her chest. "We must hurry! I don't want to miss a thing!"

William laughed again. "I think you are more anxious for Mrs. Daniels to have the baby than she is herself."

"I've been waiting for weeks!" Mary said as she pulled on her dress and pinafore. "I'm ready."

They soon arrived at the Daniels' home, and Mary and William went to work attending to the woman in labor. Several more hours passed before William indicated to Mary that the baby was emerging. Mary did everything that William instructed her to, and soon the shrill cry of a newborn was heard throughout the house.

"Thank you Dr. Hamilton, Mrs. Hamilton," the grateful mother told them. "I wasn't sure he was going to come out for a while there!"

William laughed. "They always come out, Mrs. Daniels. But sometimes they choose to take their sweet time."

On the drive back to the house, Mary was quiet. "I suppose you want to go back to sleep when we get home," William said to her.

Mary turned to him quickly. "Sleep! I can't sleep after all that. It was the most wonderful thing I've ever seen! I hope I did not get in the way."

"You didn't get in the way. You had great presence of mind throughout it all. I'm proud of you, Mary. I was worried that you were being quiet because you decided that having children is not so delightful after all."

Mary laughed. "But to see how happy Mrs. Daniels was when the baby finally came…I hope to be that happy someday. Of course I still want to have children…as many as we can! But more than that, I'd like to help at as many births as I can."

"I'll arrange it as best I can, Mary. Thank you."

The next thing Mary knew, William was waking her from a sound sleep in front of the fireplace of the sitting room. "I'm going to be late for the clinic. I overslept," he told her.

"Oh dear," Mary said, putting her hand to her forehead. "I'm sorry, William. I meant to wake you but I must have gone to sleep myself."

"The thing is, I promised to take some items to Mrs. Allen for her upcoming delivery, but I will be late for an appointment if I do. The Allen house is not so far away… easily traveled on horseback…" William trailed off.

Mary laughed at him. "I'd be happy to ride Dolly over to the Allen's. You need not worry about being late for your appointment."

"Good," William laughed. "Because I already told Sam to put the things into your saddlebags. Thank you, Mary." He kissed her goodbye and left the room. Mary changed her clothes and was soon on her way down the driveway, riding her horse Dolly.

When Mary arrived at the Allen house, the front door swung open in front of her. It was Mr. Allen. "Mrs. Hamilton, thank God you're here! Gretchen is having the baby. Is your husband with you?"

"Mrs. Allen is having the baby now?" Mary exclaimed

with wide eyes. "My husband has already gone to the clinic. We will telephone him—" but Mary was interrupted by cries from the bedroom.

"Tell the doctor that I'm pushin'!" Mrs. Allen shouted.

Mary and Mr. Allen rushed to the bedroom where the baby was already being birthed. Mary removed her jacket and worked quickly to set up the supplies. Within moments, the baby was born into Mary's trembling hands. She carefully laid the newborn boy on Mrs. Allen and covered him with a quilt. She then finished attending to the mother as she had watched William do earlier that morning. Mr. and Mrs. Allen thanked Mary over and over for arriving just in time. Mary returned to Davenport House, still in a daze over what had just happened.

"William!" she cried into the telephone. "You will never believe what I have done, all on my own!"

William laughed. "What have you done, Mary?"

"Mrs. Allen was already pushing by the time I arrived at her house!"

"What? You mean the baby has already come?"

"He is the most darling little boy I have ever seen! Not only that, it was the most magnificent feeling I've had in my life to be there and feel useful. I now am certain of what I want to do for now and always. I want to be a midwife!"

"And I think you will be a splendid one," William answered her. "I am proud of you, Mary."

Later that evening, Mary went to Clara's room to tell of her new plans. Clara was happy for her. "You will do wonderfully, Mary. You can deliver all the babies that Abigail will have after Ethan comes home."

"What about you? Don't you wish me to be there for yours as well?" Mary asked.

Clara rolled her eyes. "If I ever do get married, it will probably be too late for me."

"Now now. I saw another bouquet of roses and box of chocolates for you in the Hall. It seems your secret admirer is eager to get your attention."

Clara blushed furiously. "If only he will just say so." She bit her lip nervously. "Joe Blake is coming to dinner tonight."

"Perhaps he will finally confess," Mary giggled. "Abigail and I will have dinner in our rooms so we do not disturb you two."

"Oh please don't, Mary," objected Clara. "I would much rather you dine with us. Otherwise I will be too nervous to face him."

"Very well," Mary smiled. "I will go change now."

Mary, Abigail, Bridget, and Clara waited patiently in the drawing room for Joe Blake to arrive. Fiona had long since announced that dinner was ready to be served, but since Joe was not there, the ladies continued to wait. Mary told Abigail and Bridget about the baby born that day.

"What a perfect time for the town to have a new midwife," Abigail remarked. "I read in the paper about the shortage of doctors and nurses...because of the War..."

"It is true," Mary said quickly, observing that Abigail was becoming upset at the thought of it. "At first I thought I might volunteer with the Red Cross. They are short of volunteers, you know. But after today, I think my place is here with the women of York County."

"I don't have any time for the Red Cross while I'm leading the women's group. I would like to help, if I could."

"You are helping, Clara," Bridget offered. "Just in a different way. I've thought that if Abigail would like to volunteer for the Red Cross, I would like to go as well. We should all be doing our part to help the men who are returning."

"It is noble of you, Bridget," remarked Abigail. "I'm afraid I've been feeling sorry for myself for so long that I haven't been much use to anyone. I will take volunteering into consideration."

Clara kept her eyes fixed on the entrance to the drawing room. It was clear that Joe was not coming to dinner after all. She let out a defeated sigh. "I suppose we should go into dinner now…before it gets too cold."

On the way to the dining room, Mary walked beside Clara and spoke to her discreetly. "I'm sorry he did not come."

"Perhaps I was wrong about him caring for me."

"He may have an explanation for not attending tonight."

"You don't have to try to make me feel better, Mary," Clara whispered before she sat down at the table. "It was foolish of me to think that he could be interested in me at my age…even more foolish that I turned away the only men who were willing to marry me in the past. I suppose the secret admirer is my last chance…whoever he may be." She ate her dinner quietly before retiring to bed, feeling more tired than she had in a long time.

The next day, Clara attended a meeting at the town hall. She groaned under her breath when she observed that Mr. Collins was seated in the front row. Although he attended the meetings, he did not seem to be interested in the vote for women at all. Clara wondered why he was even there. The meeting went on as usual and the ladies stood up to leave. Clara stayed behind to tidy the room, and noticed that Mr. Collins was helping to straighten the chairs. "Thank you, Mr. Collins," Clara said reluctantly.

"I'm glad to help, Miss Davenport. I've been wanting to speak to you in private for some time anyway."

Clara looked up at him in surprise. "You wish to speak to me?"

"I was hoping you would have noticed by now, but you never seem to look at me at these meetings," Mr. Collins replied. Clara was speechless. She did not know how to respond to Mr. Collins, so he continued. "I thought that all ladies liked roses and chocolate."

"That was you?" she asked incredulously.

"Of course it was," he laughed. "Although I imagine you have a great deal of secret admirers."

"I wouldn't know about that," Clara replied. "Forgive me, Mr. Collins. I did not realize it was you who was trying to get my attention."

"Well, do I have your attention now?" he asked playfully.

"Yes," Clara said. "Um—what did you wish to say to me?"

Mr. Collins approached Clara to be closer to her. "I haven't stopped thinking about you since the day I first saw you. Since then…well Clara, I think you're the most beautiful, intelligent woman I've met. I want to marry you."

Clara could not believe her ears. It felt like she could hear the beat of her heart echo off the walls of the town hall.

"Well, do you think you might consider it?" Mr. Collins prompted. "I realize you don't know me that well, and you don't need to answer right away—"

The words spilled from her lips before she knew what she had said. "Yes, Mr. Collins. I would like to marry you."

He smiled wide and picked her up off the floor. "I was hoping you'd say that. I have to leave for New York tomorrow on business. Why don't you come with me and we'll get married while we're at it?"

Clara's eyes were wide. "You don't wish to plan for a wedding?"

Mr. Collins shook his head. "I'm sorry, Clara. I should have told you before that I'm a widower. I had a big wedding with all the extravagance already…now I just want to get married simply and start our lives together. If that isn't what you want, you don't have to come…"

"I'd love to go to New York, I just wasn't expecting any of this right now."

"I've been thinking about you for such a long time that it just seems natural for me to want to marry as soon as possible. I guess I didn't think about what a surprise it might be for you."

Clara began to laugh. "Oh, why not? I will go to New York with you. I always thought I wanted a big wedding, but now that I think of it, surprising my friends with the news might be even more thrilling!"

Mr. Collins squeezed her tightly. "Meet me here tomorrow morning and we'll drive for New York. When we come back, we'll be man and wife."

"I can hardly believe this is happening," said Clara, smiling and shaking her head. "I will be here first thing in the morning."

At the house the next day, Clara acted mysteriously about her sudden trip to New York. Sam drove her to the town hall, where Clara told him to return to the house and not worry about retrieving her that day. Mary and Abigail questioned Sam as soon as he arrived at Davenport House without Clara.

"I thought you were taking Clara to New York," Mary said, feeling confused.

"I thought so too, but she got into another car with a man I haven't seen before. Then they took off together."

"Clara is going to New York with a man? Who do you suppose he is, Mary?"

Mary looked at Abigail with wide eyes. "I wonder if Clara has discovered her real secret admirer."

Chapter 5

Clara was beaming when she returned to Davenport House the next week. Her new husband scooped her up in his arms and carried her over the threshold. Fiona observed them from the Hall and went to greet them. "Welcome back, Miss Clara," she said, taking her coat and hat.

"You may call her Mrs. Collins now, thank you very much," Mr. Collins said playfully.

Clara laughed to see Fiona gaping at them. "Fiona, may I introduce my husband, Mr. Collins. If you are this surprised to see us, Mary and Abigail will be twice as surprised!"

Fiona giggled nervously. "Yes, I'm certain they will be. They are shopping in town today, but should return soon."

"Oh," Clara frowned. "Please tell me the minute they return. My husband and I will have a walk through the gardens while we wait for them. Why don't you bring us tea and refreshments outside."

"Yes, Miss Clara. I mean, Mrs. Collins. Right away."

Fiona went to the kitchen to prepare the tray of tea and cakes, then took it outside to place on the outdoor table.

"Thank you, Fiona," Mr. Collins said. "My wife tells me you are an exceptional housekeeper."

Fiona smiled shyly and walked back to the house. Before Fiona went inside, Bridget walked out the door to greet her. "Sister, I have been looking for you. The maids said you went to the garden."

"Yes," Fiona answered. "Miss Clara has returned."

Bridget leaned to the side to see past Fiona. Then she put her hand over her heart. "Fiona—he is here! Lawrence has come to see me at last!"

Fiona turned to look into the distance. "Where is he?"

"He is there!" Bridget cried in a whisper. "How do you not see him? He is sitting with Clara at the garden table."

Fiona looked back at her sister in fright. "Bridget, that man is Mr. Collins."

"You knew he was here and you didn't tell me?" Bridget continued in a flustered tone. "Oh, I can barely stand up straight. How do I look, Fiona? I will go over to him at once."

Fiona grabbed her sister's arm and pulled her behind the bushes where they were out of sight. Bridget was displeased. "What are you doing? I want to see him this instant!"

"Miss Clara has just introduced Mr. Collins to me as her husband. They are married."

Bridget laughed. "You are mistaken. It is Lawrence here to see me. You must have misunderstood when Clara introduced him."

"There was no misunderstanding," Fiona urged. "They were married in New York while Miss Clara was away."

Bridget's countenance fell while Fiona's words began to sink in. "It's not possible," she whispered.

"I'm sorry, Bridget. Let us go back into the house." But Mr. Collins and Clara were already approaching them.

"Bridget," Clara said cheerfully. "May I present my husband, Lawrence Collins." She turned to explain to Lawrence, "Bridget is a lady's companion to Abigail."

"Very good," Lawrence said, tipping his hat toward Bridget. "I am pleased to make your acquaintance."

Clara giggled when Bridget stared speechlessly at Lawrence. "It must be a great surprise, I know. I can't wait to tell the others. We will celebrate at dinner tonight!"

After Clara and Lawrence had gone into the house, Bridget began to cry. "He acted as if he didn't know me," she sobbed to Fiona.

Fiona hugged her sister and wished she could think of words that might comfort her. "I'm terribly sorry, Bridget. I am confused and upset for you. I don't understand why Mr. Collins would treat you this way."

"Will you tell Clara that I am feeling ill and cannot come to dinner tonight?" pleaded Bridget.

"Of course I'll tell her. Let's get you to your room."

When Mary and Abigail arrived at the house just before dinner, they reacted just as surprised as everyone else. "So it was you who sent Clara all those lovely things," Mary finally said. "I was only glad that Clara shared her chocolates with me."

"Congratulations, Clara," Abigail said kindly. "Mary and I will be sure to make ourselves scarce so you may have privacy."

"There's no need for that," Lawrence said. "I must leave town in a few days, for I have business to attend to in Pittsburgh. I hope you will keep Clara the company she deserves in my absence."

"Of course we will," said Mary.

"We should all wear our best dresses to dinner tonight. I have told Mrs. Malone that we intend to celebrate!" The girls agreed and went upstairs to change for dinner.

After Abigail had put on her best dress, she walked down the hallway to Bridget's bedroom. Fiona was just coming out of the room and closing the door behind her. "Is she ready for dinner?" Abigail asked Fiona. "Clara would like to have a celebration tonight and has asked that we all wear our best clothes."

"Bridget is not well tonight, Miss Abigail," Fiona said, looking at the floor.

"What a shame," Abigail replied. "I will request that William check on her after dinner."

"Um—Miss Abigail—" Fiona stammered. "She is not ill in that way. She had some bad news today."

"Oh?" A look of realization crossed Abigail's face. "Has she finally heard about her young man?"

Fiona nodded, but did not look Abigail in the eye.

"The poor dear," Abigail remarked. "I suppose her beau is not coming for her after all."

"No he is not, Miss Abigail."

"Please bring a tray of dinner to her room," Abigail said. "I don't expect her to celebrate with us after her disappointment."

Fiona managed a smile. "Thank you, Miss Abigail. My sister and I are grateful to you for understanding."

After the celebration dinner, everyone retired to their rooms, weary from the day's events. Fiona was inspecting the maids' progress on the upstairs rooms before she could retire for bed. Just as she was about to go down the servants' stairs, she heard a voice whisper from behind her. "Fiona!"

Fiona turned around to face Lawrence. "What can I do for you, Mr. Collins?" she asked quickly.

"I just wondered which of these bedrooms belongs to Bridget. Boy, this house is big!"

Fiona was appalled at his question. "If you wish to speak to Bridget, you must wait until the morning. Everyone has retired to bed already."

Lawrence sighed in disappointment. "I suppose she told you about how I used to see her in Philadelphia."

"She mentioned it," Fiona answered curtly.

"Well, I just want to talk to her—clear up any misunderstanding there may have been today." Lawrence scanned the bedroom doors in the hallway.

"Like I said, if you wish to speak to her, it will have to wait until the morning. Good night, Mr. Collins."

The next morning, Clara, Mary, and Abigail had breakfast alone. "I assumed you would be having breakfast in bed today," Abigail remarked to Clara.

"Lawrence had to go into town this morning, and I wanted to see you all anyway," answered Clara.

"I have a birth to attend, so I cannot stay," Mary said, rising from her seat.

"Hope all goes well, Mary," Abigail said kindly. "I am going to look in on Serena today. I thought I would offer to care for the children if she wanted to leave the house."

"Very well," sighed Clara. "Then I am going back to bed. I am exhausted after all the travel and excitement. Have a good day, ladies." Clara went upstairs and lay in bed, but felt restless. She got dressed again and decided to take a walk in the gardens.

"Clara?" called a voice.

"Joe!" she answered in surprise. "I was not sure if we would see you again."

Joe cringed in embarrassment. "I heard you just got back from New York. I've been wanting to tell you how sorry I was for missing your dinner. The cows got out that night, and…well, you know how that goes."

"It's alright, Mr. Blake." Clara could feel her heart pounding in her chest. Feelings from the past washed over her, and she remembered again how it felt when she thought that Joe was her secret admirer.

"Miss Davenport," he began nervously, looking into her eyes. "I've been wanting to ask if it's alright for me to call on you."

"Oh," Clara felt her cheeks turning pink. "There is something I should tell you. You see, I am Mrs. Collins now. I was married just this week."

Joe's tan face went pale. "You were?"

Clara nodded with a smile. "It all happened so fast. None of us expected it."

Joe stood there awkwardly. "I see. Then I wish you well, Mrs. Collins."

"Thank you, Mr. Blake." Clara watched Joe walk away with his head down. She felt her heart sink into her stomach and she suddenly panicked, wondering if she had acted too soon and made a terrible mistake. She went back into the house and lay in her bed, soon drifting off to sleep. With her eyes still closed, she heard a sound like someone had entered the room. She heard the drawer to the bureau open and close, and she looked just in time to see Lawrence exiting the bedroom. Clara looked at the bureau curiously. She got out of bed and opened the top drawer of the bureau. Hidden under some handkerchiefs was a velvet box. Clara smiled when she realized it must be jewelry. She peeked inside and gasped in delight at the costly diamond necklace. Clara quickly closed the box and slid it back under the handkerchiefs in the drawer to make it look as if she had never seen the necklace at all.

At the Valentis' farmhouse, Serena returned from her day in town. "Thank you again, Abigail," she said gratefully. "I don't know what I would do without you!"

"It is no trouble at all," Abigail replied with a smile.

Serena removed several colorful bows from her handbag. "I thought Gabriella would like some of these for her hair," she said. "This one is for Angelina. I plan to send it in the post for her."

"You must miss her terribly," Abigail said gently.

Serena nodded. "I wish I could visit her. My friends say I may visit at any time—" she paused and shook her head. "Even if I could afford it, I cannot leave until Phillip returns."

"Have you heard from him?" asked Abigail.

"No," Serena replied. "I have written to him, but I do not know if my letters ever reached him. Have you heard from your husband?"

Abigail suddenly became downcast. "I have not heard a word. I wish I could have told him goodbye properly. I feel terribly guilty for how I behaved the week he had to leave. I only hope he has forgiven me for it."

"Surely he understands," Serena offered. "The War can't last for much longer. The men might return at any day."

Abigail tried to smile. "I pray every day for the War to end so our men can come home. I nearly forgot to tell you that Clara had a surprise wedding in New York. Now she and Mary are at home with their husbands, and I am lonely in the house without mine. I do have a companion at least. She is a dear girl, but is going through a heart-break just now." Abigail paused, then looked up at Serena. "Thank you for talking to me. I think I feel better now." She collected her things and returned to the house, think-ing of more ways that she may help Serena.

The following day, Clara was preparing for a meeting at the town hall. "Are you certain you don't want to come with me?" she asked Lawrence.

"I'd rather stay here, Sweetheart," he answered, kissing her goodbye. "It's probably time I familiarize myself with the house."

Clara smiled. "Then I hope you will miss me dreadfully all day."

"Of course I will," Lawrence told her. After Clara left, Lawrence walked down the hallway straight to Bridget's bedroom and knocked on the door.

"Come in," Bridget answered from the other side. "Lawrence!" she cried when he entered the room. "What are you doing in here?"

"You said 'come in'," he answered playfully.

"I never thought it was you—you can't be in here! What if someone sees?"

Lawrence shrugged. "Clara has a meeting in town, and I wanted to see you. I want to explain."

Bridget looked skeptical. "You want to explain why you jilted me and married the very woman whose house I live in?"

"It was the only way, Bridget. The only way we could be together."

"What do you mean by that?" she demanded. "We are not together! You are married to the lady of the house!"

"It's just an arrangement. I had no way to pay for my mother's hospital bills, and Clara has paid it all for me now. I could not have earned the money on my own, no matter how much I worked."

"So you married Clara," Bridget said disgustedly. "Even though you led me to believe that you wanted me."

"I do want to be with you," Lawrence said, stepping close to her and taking her hand. "It's why I came to live here. Clara knows I don't love her. She was eager to be married, and I needed funds for my mother. It's only an arrangement. Not like the feelings I have for you."

Bridget stared at him in disbelief. "How do you think Clara would feel if she knew you were in my room saying these things to me right now?"

Lawrence shrugged again. "She knows our marriage was only for convenience. She can't expect me to live without a mistress. It's the way things are done in many houses, Bridget."

Bridget looked at Lawrence in horror. "Did you tell Clara about me?"

"No," he laughed. "But she won't mind as long as we are discreet."

Bridget crossed her arms over her chest. "I'm not sure what to think about anything you say now, Lawrence."

"Then let me prove that I mean what I say." He took her by the hand and led her into the bedroom he shared with Clara. He opened the top drawer of the bureau and removed the velvet box.

Bridget looked around the room uncomfortably. "I don't think we should be in here," she said.

"Then show me to a room that no one uses or looks

in," Lawrence said with a laugh. Bridget reluctantly led him to one of the guest rooms at the back of the house.

"This room was vacant for as long as I worked here," Bridget said quietly. "I think it is too far from the stairs and other rooms to be desirable."

"Then it will be a room for just you and me—our secret place," Lawrence said, opening the box and removing the diamond necklace. "I bought this for you when I went to town yesterday."

Bridget stared in awe. "Lawrence, this looks awfully expensive."

"Then you can know how much I care for you," he said, clasping it around her neck. "Will you meet me in our secret room tonight after everyone else has gone to sleep?"

Bridget looked into his eyes and began to remember how much she had once wanted to be alone with him. "I—I don't know," she said. "I have to think about it."

"I'll be here. Hopefully it doesn't take you too long to think about it," he said with a wink. Bridget nodded, then left the room quickly, hoping that no one in the house had seen them upstairs together.

Later that afternoon, Fiona brought a tray of tea to the upstairs sitting room. Bridget was seated alone in front of the fireplace. "Are you feeling any better today, Bridget?" Fiona asked softly.

"I'm not sure," she answered, her gaze fixed on the fireplace.

"Will Miss Abigail be taking tea with you?" Fiona asked.

"She is still with Serena Valenti," Bridget answered stoically. Fiona poured tea for Bridget and brought it to her on a saucer.

Fiona gasped when she saw the necklace. "Are those real diamonds?"

"Of course," Bridget answered. "It was a gift."

Fiona shook her head in wonder. "Miss Abigail was very generous. I can't imagine how much such a piece would have cost her!"

"It wasn't from Abigail," Bridget said quietly, not looking Fiona in the eye.

Fiona's heart sank. "Tell me it was not given to you by Clara's new husband."

"He doesn't love her anyway. He loves me," Bridget replied in defense.

"I suppose that is what he told you," Fiona said angrily. "Why would he marry her if he loves you?"

"Just because he has a rich wife doesn't mean he can't have a mistress."

Fiona gasped. "You can't be serious! Bridget, this isn't like you. You're too good for this! And you mustn't wear that diamond necklace around Miss Clara—it's not right!"

"You are the one who works for her, not me."

"You are living in Miss Clara's house!"

"Who are you to tell me what to do, anyway?" Bridget demanded, hot tears stinging her eyes.

"Bridget, you can't love someone who you have no chance of being with!"

"And what about you? When I last worked at this house, you were head over heels for Mr. Valenti. I never told you that you shouldn't be with him, even though everyone knows that he has been in love with Abigail from the beginning, and would marry her the moment he had the chance!"

The sisters heard a gasp from the doorway. When they looked to see who had just entered the room, they were aghast to see Abigail, who had returned from the Valentis'.

Her expression was grave. "Fiona, I need to have a word with Bridget, please."

"Yes, Miss Abigail." Fiona hurried out of the room.

Bridget cowered in front of Abigail. "I'm desperately sorry. I didn't realize that anyone had come into the room!"

"And what if it was one of the others? What if it was Ethan? What do you think it would do for my family and reputation if someone had heard you talking this way?"

"I apologize with all my heart. I should not have said it at all!"

"No, you should not have," Abigail replied sternly. "I think you should go to your room now while I decide what to do about it."

Chapter 6

The next morning before breakfast, Abigail was styling her hair at her vanity table when Fiona entered the room. "Miss Abigail, I must speak with you."

"What is it?"

"It's Bridget. She has left."

"When will she be back?"

Fiona looked distressed to answer. "Bridget is not coming back. She went to volunteer with the Red Cross."

Abigail cringed. "I hope I was not too harsh with her."

"I don't think you were. My sister was very sorry to be leaving you, but she said that it was time she did her part for the cause."

Abigail nodded. "I see. Thank you for informing me, Fiona."

Abigail was quiet at the dining table that morning. Mary asked why Bridget had not been coming to dine with them. "She left to volunteer for the Red Cross this morning," Abigail replied.

Clara looked at her bewildered. "It seems rather sudden. Do you intend to find another companion?"

"No," Abigail said quietly. "I will be leaving the house too. You see, Serena Valenti has family who she wishes to visit in Pittsburgh, and I will stay at the farmhouse with the children while she is away."

"It's kind of you, Abigail. At least you will not be far away from the house and we may still see each other often," said Mary.

Abigail nodded. "I know that you are quite busy with delivering babies now, and I don't wish to get in the way of the newlyweds."

Clara laughed. "You are never in the way. Lawrence has to leave town on business, and I will be spending more time at the town hall this week anyway."

Abigail quietly responded, "It appears like we all have something to pass the time while we wait for our men to return."

She arrived at Serena's house directly after breakfast. Serena greeted her cheerfully, but was confused when she saw Abigail's traveling case. "Good morning. Are you leaving town?"

"I am not, but you are," Abigail stated as she entered the house. "You are going to visit Angelina while I stay here with the children."

Serena stared at her in astonishment. "You would do this for me?"

Abigail smiled and handed her an envelope. "It is twenty-five dollars. It should be enough for your travel."

Serena's eyes were wide. "More than enough, I should think. I can't take your money, Abigail. It's too much."

"Nonsense. I never know what to spend my money on anyway." She kissed Serena on the cheek. "Now go pack your things and get ready. Sam is waiting outside in the car. He will take you to the train station."

Serena hugged Abigail tightly. "You are too good to be true! Thank you!"

After Serena left the house, Gabriella and Donnie reacted in delight when Abigail explained that she would be staying at the farmhouse. "You're nicer than our Aunt Serena," Gabriella said dramatically. "She never lets us have sweets."

Abigail laughed. "We will not have too many sweets while I am here," she clarified. "But I am certain we can still have a good time." Abigail settled in with the children, content in knowing that Serena was on her way to see her daughter.

Later that afternoon, Sam drove Clara to the bank in Yorktown. The clerk cordially greeted Clara. "Mrs. Collins, how may I help you today?"

Clara smiled to herself. She was still becoming accustomed to being called Mrs. Collins, and it took a moment to realize it was she who was being addressed. "Good afternoon, Mabel. I would like to make a withdrawal. One hundred, please."

Mabel furrowed her brow. "Mrs. Collins, the balance of your account with us is only ten dollars."

"Impossible," Clara responded. "My balance was at five thousand after my last deposit, and I have not made a withdrawal since."

"I know you haven't, Madam. But Mr. Collins has."

"My husband came here?"

Mabel nodded. "He withdrew all the funds except for the ten dollars. I have the receipt just here." Clara looked over the receipt and felt her heart sink when she saw

Lawrence's signature at the bottom. She stared at the page until all the words began to run together. Mabel spoke to Clara again after the awkward silence. "Mrs. Collins? Do you wish to withdraw the ten dollars?"

"It is not enough to pay the servants," Clara finally said. "I must pay their wages today."

"I'm sorry, Mrs. Collins. Perhaps Mr. Collins has already paid them. He did mention that he would be managing the finances for the house now that you are married."

Clara swallowed the lump in her throat. "Thank you, Mabel. I will simply speak to him later. He must have forgotten to tell me before he left on business."

Mabel nodded. "Have a good afternoon, Mrs. Collins."

Clara's knees felt weak as she stumbled to the car where Sam was waiting for her. "Are you alright, Mrs. Collins?" he asked as he helped her into the car.

"I'm fine. Sam—did you receive your wages this morning from Mr. Collins?"

"No Ma'am," he replied.

Clara took a deep breath. "Take me home, quickly."

At the Valentis' farmhouse, Abigail was preparing dinner for the children when there was a knock at the front door. "Abigail, it's me," Clara called from the other side.

"Good evening, Clara," Abigail greeted when she opened the door. "What brings you here?"

Clara held a satchel in her hands and seemed distressed as she spoke. "I need to speak with you."

Abigail motioned for her to sit at the small kitchen table. "You look pale," she said in concern. "Are you feeling alright?"

Clara shook her head. "I'm sorry to ask you this, but I wonder if I may borrow one hundred dollars. I must pay the servants' wages today, and my bank account is nearly empty."

"Of course you may borrow the money," replied Abigail. "Are your tenants late on their rent?"

Tears began to roll down Clara's face. "I had five thousand dollars in the bank—but Lawrence has taken nearly all of it. I only found out because I went to make a withdrawal today and the clerk told me that my account had only ten dollars left."

Abigail put her hand over her heart. "Five thousand is a fortune. What would he need that kind of money for?"

Clara shook her head sorrowfully. "Oh Abigail, I'm afraid that I acted hastily with Lawrence. I feared that it would be the last time I was made an offer, but the truth is, I don't know anything about him or what he could need this money for. He never said a word to me about visiting the bank. I must wait until he returns to confront him... which is why I need to ask another favor of you." Clara placed the satchel on the kitchen table and slid it toward Abigail. "These are ledgers of my investments that Lawrence has not seen yet. After today—I am afraid for him to know about them—until we get this matter of the five thousand sorted out. Would you be able to keep them safe for me?"

"Here at the farmhouse?"

"Yes. Lawrence must have already searched the library at the house if he discovered the information on my bank account. I usually kept these ledgers hidden in case we were ever burglarized. I am not ready to tell Lawrence that I have them."

Abigail smiled compassionately at Clara. "Of course I will keep them safe here." She rose from her seat and opened the trapdoor to the cellar. Clara handed her the satchel and Abigail took it down the stairs and placed it on a shelf next to the canned vegetables. "Your ledgers will be just down here if you ever need them."

"Thank you, Abigail," Clara said. "This is the most embarrassed I've ever been. I promise to pay you back the hundred dollars just as soon as I can." Abigail felt sorry for Clara as she left the farmhouse.

Abigail finished making supper for the children and it was nearing time for bed. Gabriella and Donnie asked her to lie on the bed with them until they fell asleep, and Abigail agreed. She watched the stars through the window of the room when she suddenly caught a glimpse of headlight beams from a passing car. She wondered if Lawrence had returned from his business trip. Abigail hoped that he and Clara would resolve the misunderstanding with the money. But when she heard the front door of the farmhouse creak open, Abigail bolted upright in the bed. She heard heavy footsteps cross the kitchen floor. The footsteps grew louder as they came down the hallway.

Abigail felt her heart pounding in her ears, and remembered the rifle hanging over the fireplace in the sitting room. But whoever was in the house was between Abigail and the rifle. She drew a sharp breath and stared in fright as the door to the children's room slowly opened in front of her. She saw the silhouette of a man standing in the doorway.

"Abigail?" came Phillip Valenti's bewildered voice.

Before Abigail knew what she was doing, she had run to Phillip and thrown her arms around him. "Is Ethan with you?" she cried frantically.

"No," he answered quietly. "It's only me."

"Oh," she answered, still trembling and hugging him

tightly. "I was so afraid when I heard footsteps coming to the children's room. I didn't know it was you!"

"I was anxious to see them."

"Oh—of course—I'm sorry," she stammered as she backed away. She watched him lean over Gabriella and Donnie so he could kiss their sleeping faces. Abigail went into the kitchen and turned on the light, hoping to find something for Phillip to eat. When he came out of the hallway, Abigail noticed that he limped and walked with a cane.

"Where is Serena?" he asked.

"She is in Pittsburgh visiting Angelina. I offered to watch the children until she returned," Abigail explained.

"Thank you," he said wearily, and winced in pain as he lowered himself onto a kitchen chair.

Abigail set a plate of cold meats and cheeses in front of him. "Have you seen Ethan since training camp?"

"We fought together in France," he answered. "I got hurt two weeks ago and they took me to a medic camp. I didn't see Ethan again after that day."

Abigail frowned. "Do you think he is alright?"

Phillip forced a smile but avoided the question. "Haven't you heard from him?"

Abigail shook her head. "I haven't received a single letter."

"The letters must have been lost in the mail. I watched him write to you a dozen times," Phillip told her.

Abigail felt her heartbeat quicken. "Did he truly?" Then she noticed that Phillip's plate was empty. She took the plate to the counter and served another helping. Phillip was wincing in pain as he reached down to unlace his boots. "Oh, I can take them off for you," she offered.

Phillip chuckled. "I hate to have you do it for me, but I might be in too much pain to argue."

"I'll send William over first thing in the morning to have a look at you," Abigail told him. She carefully removed his boots and took them out to the front porch. When she returned the kitchen, Phillip was already sleeping soundly in the chair.

At Davenport House, Clara awoke to the sound of the telephone ringing. Her heart raced when she imagined what sort of call would come at this time of night. She ran to the library and breathlessly answered the telephone.

"Clara," Lawrence's voice came from the other end.

"Lawrence! Is everything alright? Are you on your way home?"

"No, that's what I called to tell you. My mother is ill and I'll be staying with her in Pittsburgh for a while. I don't know how much longer she has left."

"Oh, I see," Clara said gently. "I'm sorry about your mother." She paused for a moment before continuing. "Lawrence, there was a matter at the bank when I went to make a withdrawal. The clerk said you had taken all the money."

"Well, I left you ten dollars," he replied.

"But where has the money gone? I've spent years saving it, and we need it to pay the taxes as well as the servants' wages."

"Don't worry, I still have it," he assured her. "I brought it in case I needed it for my business trip or for my mother. Do you want me to send you the money?"

"Yes, please," Clara answered quickly.

"I will drop it in the post tomorrow," he said. "I'll telephone again when I'm coming home."

"Thank you, Lawrence. I hope your mother gets well."

"I hope so too. Goodbye, Clara."

After Clara hung up the phone, she saw that Abigail had just entered the house. "Has Serena returned already?" she asked.

"No," Abigail replied. "But Phillip has."

Clara gasped. "How wonderful! We must invite him for dinner and celebrate his return."

Abigail hesitated. "He is injured. I promised to tell William to look in on him in the morning. Why are you awake at this time of night?"

"I had a telephone call from Lawrence. It was all just a misunderstanding…with the money. Lawrence is posting it to me tomorrow," she explained.

"Oh, thank goodness. I'm glad you were able to get it sorted, Clara."

"You can bring the ledgers back from the farmhouse now. I'm not worried anymore," Clara told her.

Abigail giggled. "I will be sure to retrieve them from the root cellar the next time I visit."

Early the next morning, William went to the farmhouse to see Phillip. Gabriella answered the door cheerfully. "Dr. Hamilton! My papa is home," she told William.

He smiled at the little girl. "So I hear. May I come in and see him?"

"Sure!" she said, opening the door wide. Phillip was reclined in the sitting room.

"Abigail said that you might need your leg checked out," William told him.

"I'm afraid it hurts worse now than it did when I left France," Phillip replied.

William rolled back the pant leg and removed the bandage. "You've got a bad infection," he said solemnly.

"I figured as much."

"I'm going to clean it now and put on a fresh bandage. Get as much rest and water as you can. We need this infection to go away so your leg can heal," William explained. He turned to the children. "Why don't you two play outside while I get your papa's leg cleaned up?" The children went out the back door and William turned to Phillip. "I'm sorry, but this is going to hurt. I've seen a lot of injuries like this at the clinic now that the wounded soldiers are being sent home. Sometimes a man gets lucky and the infection heals. Other times…"

"I know," Phillip answered, his voice catching in his throat.

"I'll do everything I can to save it. But if it gets much worse…it's better to lose a limb than your life."

Phillip nodded that he understood, clenching his jaw in pain while William cleaned the wound. The new bandage was soon placed on, and William returned to the house to find Abigail.

"Abigail, I've seen Phillip this morning and now I need to get to the clinic. Do you think you can return to the farmhouse and help with the children for a few more days?" he asked her.

"Yes, of course. Is Phillip alright?"

"He is going to need help around the house. If he starts feeling ill and feverish, call me right away."

"Oh dear. Is it that serious?" Abigail prodded.

William looked at her sorrowfully. "His leg will likely need to come off."

Abigail covered her mouth with her hand. "How terrible. I did not realize he was that bad."

"He puts on a brave face, but make no mistake, he's in a great deal of pain."

Abigail nodded solemnly. "I will go over at once."

When William arrived at the clinic that morning, one of the nurses greeted him urgently. "Jake Robinson is back with a bad fever. We have no more anesthetic."

William felt sick to his stomach. "We'll have to amputate without it. Prepare him for surgery right away." William opened the curtain to see the man writhing in pain. "Jake, we've done all we can for you and your leg hasn't improved. We need to operate today."

"No!" he cried, his teeth chattering from the chills. "I won't let you take it off! Just fix it, Doctor. You can't leave me without my leg!"

"I'm sorry, but the infection will kill you if we wait any longer."

"No it won't! You're lying!" he shouted through his teeth. "You won't fix my leg up because—because you're one of them!"

William remained calm. "I know you're upset—"

Jake Robinson reached into his boot and pulled out a knife, holding it menacingly in front of William. "You're one of them. You won't help me. I'll go to the witch in the woods if I have to, but I'll never come back here." He finally hobbled out of the clinic.

William felt his heart racing as he watched him leave. The nurse came alongside him. "Are you alright, Dr. Hamilton? Should I call the police?"

"No need," William replied. "With the severity of that infection, he'll be dead by tomorrow."

On his way back to the house that night, William stopped by the farmhouse to have another look at Phillip's leg. William's expression was grim when he looked under the bandage. "How you're not screaming in pain right now is beyond me."

Phillip shrugged. "I might if I thought screaming would help."

"I'm going to bring my instruments with me when I return from the clinic tomorrow. If your leg still looks like this by the evening, I'll have to take it off."

"Alright," Phillip sighed in defeat. "I'm luckier than some men who lost both legs or arms. I suppose I just have to remember that."

"The beds at the clinic are full and I don't want to move you anyway. Mary will care for your children at the house and we will operate here."

Phillip nodded in a agreement. "I'll be praying that my leg looks better by tomorrow."

The next day after breakfast, Abigail spoke to William before he left for the clinic. "Is there anything I can do to help with tonight?"

"I can't spare any nurses from the clinic, but I need someone to help me hold him down. I was going to ask Sam…"

Abigail shuddered. "I don't wish my brother to see such a thing. I know where to find everything in the farmhouse, and I can help to hold Phillip down while you operate."

"Are you sure, Abigail?"

She nodded. "I want to help. I intend to volunteer for the Red Cross once Serena returns. I'm stronger than I look."

William smiled. "I have no doubt about that." He held out a glass bottle to her. "Give him this at about 5 o'clock."

"What is it?"

"Whiskey. Make sure he takes all of it. Unfortunately, we'll be working without anesthetic. The clinic ran out last week and there's nowhere to get more."

Abigail felt tears stinging her eyes, but spoke confidently, "I'll be sure he takes all of it."

At 5 o'clock, William was on his way out of the clinic with his medical bag and operating instruments. He heard a voice calling his name from down the street. "Hey Doc!"

William was astounded to see Jake Robinson walking out of one of the shops and seeming cheerful. He hobbled over to William while supporting himself on his cane. "I'm sorry about all that from yesterday. I know you were only trying to help. I was just scared of losing my leg!"

"I had you figured for a goner, Jake. I can't believe the fever cleared and you don't even seem worse for the wear."

"No Sir, I went to see the witch like I said. She put some potion on my leg, and as you can see, it's almost as good as new."

"I don't understand. You mean to tell me that a witch healed you?"

"Yes Sir. Take a look if you'd like." Jake pulled back the bandage to reveal a thick layer of green ointment over the wound.

"I'm astonished," William confessed. "What did the woman give you?"

Jake shrugged. "All I know is, I get to keep my leg. You can ask her if you'd like. Greta Jenkins is her name."

"The name sounds familiar. Did she used to be the county midwife?" William asked.

"That's the one," Jake said confidently.

William was intrigued. "Where can I find Miss Jenkins?" He received directions from Jake and was soon driving away from Yorktown to visit the alleged witch in the woods.

At the Valentis' farmhouse, Abigail watched the clock strike 5, then gave the bottle of whiskey to Phillip as she was instructed. "William said that you should take the whole bottle, so don't be shy on my account. The children are safe with Mary and all you need to do now is relax," she told him.

Phillip was embarrassed. "It seems improper to drink all this in front of a lady."

Abigail giggled. "Don't worry about that. I'll just be here reading my book while we wait for William to come."

William pulled his car over on the side of the road that Jake told him about. He climbed out of the car and began hiking up a treed hill, hoping he had come to the right place. After walking for several minutes, he could see a small log cabin in the distance. "Hello!" he called loudly. It was the safest greeting when one approached a remote house likely to be stocked with rifles. A woman emerged from the cabin and walked in his direction.

"Miss Jenkins, I'm—"

"I know who you are," Greta interrupted. "I can guess why you've come, too."

"Oh?"

"You want to tell me to stay away from your patients," she said bitterly.

William raised his eyebrows in surprise. "No Ma'am, that's not why I have come at all."

The woman looked at him skeptically. "I don't trust doctors much after what the last one did to me. He ran me out of town just to get more business for himself. I can't show my face again because of what they called me."

William did not know how to respond to that. "I don't wish to bother you, Miss Jenkins. I only want to know what it was you used for Jake Robinson's injury. I've never seen an infection clear so fast, and he claims it was because of a potion you used on him."

"It's plantain," she muttered. "I mixed it up into an ointment for open sores. It keeps infections down."

"Would you mind showing me how you mixed it up? I'm happy to pay."

Instead of answering him, Greta walked back into the cabin. William hoped he had not offended her, and blew a sigh of relief when she came back out with a large pail. "Here, take the rest of it with you."

"Thank you, Miss Jenkins. How much do you want for it?"

"I don't want your money, Dr. Hamilton. My only condition is that you don't tell anyone who or where you got it from. It's for your safety as much as it is mine. I only wish Jake wasn't such a blabbermouth."

"Again, I thank you," William said. Greta went back into the cabin and closed the door, indicating to William that it was time for him to leave. He carried the pail back to his car and began the long drive home.

Abigail watched the clock on the wall at the farmhouse. It was 7 o'clock, and she wondered what could be taking William so long. Phillip looked at her sleepily. "Is it time yet?" he asked.

"William should be here any moment," she replied.

"You know the last time I saw Ethan, it was when I got this," he slurred, pointing to his leg. "He dragged me out of the line of fire…saved my life…I'd be dead right now if he didn't get me out of there."

Abigail began to feel herself getting choked up. She tried to save her strength for the ordeal yet to come.

"You know what the last thing he said to me was? We were supposed to leave the trenches to a place where we were going to get shot. He stopped me before I went out there and made me promise to take care of you and Mary if he didn't come back."

Abigail held back painful tears. "Perhaps we can talk about this another time," she said gently.

Phillip leaned back in his chair. "I thought he must be the happiest man in the world. I would be the happiest man in the world if I had you for a wife."

Abigail looked at the clock again and sighed impatiently.

Phillip continued, "I know you turned me down when I asked, but I always thought how nice it would be to get married and have babies with you."

Abigail quickly rose from her seat and went to the kitchen for a glass of water. Then she opened the front door to look outside, but there was no sign of William. "I think you should try to rest now, Phillip, and…stop talking."

"I'm sorry, did I talk too much?" he sighed. "I didn't mean to upset you. I thought I would have lots of babies with Sofia. She had Gabriella right after we got married. Then Donnie came along. Then, she was about to have another—" Phillip stopped talking and began crying into his hands. "But that one died with her. We could have had lots of babies if only she had lived."

Abigail closed her eyes in relief when William came through the front door. "Thank goodness you are here. He had the bottle two hours ago. I was afraid you weren't going to come."

"I changed my mind about operating tonight," William said, walking past her to Phillip. "There's something I want to try first." He pulled back the bandage to expose the wound, then he reached into the pail and began smearing Greta's ointment over it.

Phillip stopped crying and began to laugh. "Thank you, Dr. Hamilton. It feels so much better now that my leg is gone. Phew! I'm sorry I had to shoot at those Germans. I hope they were no relations of yours."

William ignored him and was about to apply a fresh bandage, but he observed that debris began to come to the surface of the wound. He removed as much as he could see, then finally wrapped the bandage around the leg. Phillip had fallen asleep in the chair and Abigail watched it all with wide eyes. William turned to her to explain. "There was still debris in his leg that was keeping it from healing. I think this ointment brought it out somehow."

"Do you think the infection might heal after all?" she asked.

"We can only wait and see. The last thing I want to do is amputate if there is any chance of healing. I'll have to keep watch of him through the night. If he begins to develop chills or fever, then we are back to square one."

"Go home to Mary," Abigail said kindly. "I know you hardly see her anymore. I will stay here and keep watch." William gratefully left the farmhouse and Abigail returned to the sitting room to read her book. Phillip snored loudly in the chair across from her.

Abigail awoke suddenly to the sound of clanging dishes in the kitchen. It was morning, and she was still in her chair with the book in her lap.

"Sorry about the noise," Phillip said nervously. "I was just trying to make some coffee."

"I can make the coffee," Abigail offered. "How do you feel?"

Phillip laughed. "Well, I sure was surprised to wake up this morning to two legs instead of one. I guess the doctor never made it over last night. My leg feels fine, but my head…"

"That would be the whiskey," Abigail smiled. "But you don't feel chills or fever?"

"No, just a headache," he confirmed.

William knocked on the door and entered just then. "How's the leg?" he asked quickly.

Phillip returned to the chair in the kitchen and showed him the bandage. William had a look and breathed in relief. "Well, what do you know. It looks better already."

Phillip laughed. "I can walk from here to the kitchen without groaning."

"That's just what I hoped to hear." William then turned to Abigail with a grin. "I nearly forgot, Mary said to tell you that you had a letter in the post."

Abigail began to tremble. "Is it from Ethan?"

"Sure looks that way—" William started to say, but Abigail had already run out the open door of the farmhouse.

Chapter 7

Abigail,

I don't know if you are getting any of these letters, but I want you to know that I am well. I haven't stopped thinking about you since I left the house. I love you more than anything and can't wait to hold you in my arms again.

Ethan

Abigail held the letter against her heart. "He writes to say that he is well, Mary." Tears fell down her cheeks.

Mary smiled and sat next to her. "I can't tell you how relieved I am to hear that. I've been so worried, and I know you have too."

"It is the most wonderful page of paper in all the world."

"I agree," Mary giggled. "Perhaps we may frame it to hang on the wall."

Abigail laughed, holding her stomach. "It feels good to laugh and be merry again. I had forgotten what it feels like!"

"Any news of when he'll be home?" Mary asked.

"No, unfortunately," sighed Abigail. "But how much longer can this War last? It must be nearly over by now."

Clara entered the sitting room where Mary and Abigail were talking. The color had drained from her face. "Abigail," she said in dismay. "There is a messenger at the front door to see you. He is from the army."

Abigail exchanged looks with Mary and could see the worry in her face. "Oh—I wonder what it could be about." She rose from her seat and left Mary and Clara in the sitting room.

"Did he say why he was here?" Mary asked, her eyes wide.

"He wouldn't say to me, but you should brace yourself, Mary. I think there is only one reason the army sends a messenger to the house."

Mary covered her heart and held her breath. She and Clara waited in the sitting room for Abigail to return. They did not see or hear her from her for several minutes, so they went downstairs and found her sitting on the bottom steps of the staircase.

"What did the messenger say?" Mary asked.

Abigail stared blankly as if in a daze. "It's a mistake," she told her. "He came to deliver this message, but it has to be a mistake." She handed the paper to Mary.

Mrs. Smith,

We regret very much to inform you that your husband E.J. Smith, No. 5932 of this Company was killed in action on the night of September 5. He now lies in a soldier's grave where he fell. We sympathize with you in your loss and honor your husband for doing his duty and giving his life for his country.

In true sympathy,
Captain T. Morris

Clara hurried to the telephone and called the clinic. "William, Mary needs you. A messenger from the army was just here—about Ethan."

"I'll be right there," William's voice answered.

Clara returned the phone to its cradle and went to see Abigail and Mary, who remained seated on the bottom steps of the staircase.

"I don't think this letter was meant for me," Abigail was saying. "Ethan just wrote to say that he is well...you saw it yourself. Perhaps this message was meant for another Mrs. Smith. It is a common name."

Mary was silent as tears streamed into her lap. Abigail turned to face her. "Don't cry, Mary. Ethan is well, I just know it. I would feel it in my heart if something happened to him. It's a mistake...that is all."

Clara looked between Abigail and Mary. No one knew what to say. Finally Clara cleared her throat and spoke, "William is on his way home."

"Thank you, Clara," Mary said mournfully. She slowly rose to her feet and went up the stairs to her room.

Abigail watched her walk away. "Poor Mary. She

doesn't realize that these mistakes happen sometimes. I'm going to the farmhouse to tell Phillip that I've had a letter from Ethan. He will be glad to hear that Ethan is alright."

Clara stared at Abigail in confusion. Abigail hardly seemed to notice that Clara was standing there. She left the staircase and went out the front door on her way to the farmhouse. Phillip greeted her with a smile. "You don't have to come help with the children today. I can manage," he told her at the front door. "I sure do appreciate your help this week."

"I was glad to help," Abigail replied. "I received a letter from Ethan today. He wrote to say that he has written other letters, but this is the only one that reached me. Then an army messenger came to the door today to deliver another letter." Abigail gave him the paper from the Captain.

"Oh," Phillip said quietly. As soon as he read the words *September 5*, he froze and held his breath. In his mind, he was in the trenches again, feeling the piercing pain from the shrapnel in his leg. He heard the voice of the general barking orders to the others and the sound of artillery shells vibrated through his chest. He looked into Ethan's face as he made him a promise, then everything went black again.

"Phillip, do you hear me?" Abigail was asking him frantically. "It's possible that the letter is a mistake, right?"

Phillip snapped back to the present. "What did you ask?"

Abigail was frustrated as she repeated herself. "I asked if it's possible for this letter to have reached me by accident. Perhaps they got the names switched or, I don't know, but mistakes happen with letters like these, don't they?"

Phillip looked at her in sorrow. "I suppose it can happen, sometimes…"

Abigail breathed in relief. "Thank you," she said, abruptly

taking the paper from his hand and leaving to return to the house. When she entered the Hall, she saw that Clara was there speaking with Sam. They both looked at her.

"I'm sorry, Abby," Sam told her, hanging his head.

Abigail looked angrily at Clara. "You had to get my brother all worried over nothing. I'm telling you, it's a mistake! Even Phillip agrees with me. I'm certain there is another letter on it's way, taking back everything that was said in this one. We only have to wait for it. Go back to work, Sam, and don't worry about me. I'll be upstairs reading my book in the sitting room today." Abigail stumbled up the stairs and closed the double doors to the sitting room.

Sam looked at the floor sadly. "She did the same thing when our ma died. Abby said we shouldn't bury her until we knew for sure that she was no longer with us…but we all knew."

Clara looked helplessly at Sam. "What should we do about her?"

"Just give her time, I guess. The news might sink in when the letter that she's waiting for never comes."

A week went by, but Abigail would not change her mind about the news of Ethan. Mary wore her black mourning dress and spoke to Abigail in her bedroom. "It is time for us to arrange a memorial service for Ethan, since we cannot have a proper burial for him," Mary said quietly.

Abigail stubbornly crossed her arms over her chest. "I won't have any part of it, Mary."

"If you won't think of it as being for you, then think of it as being for me. He was my brother. I want to honor him properly."

"Such a thing would bring bad luck on us and may

even kill Ethan for real," Abigail said, then returned her gaze to the book she was reading.

Mary left the room and made her way to the farmhouse. Phillip appeared depressed when he answered the door. "I'm sorry for your loss, Mrs. Hamilton," he said, bowing his head.

"May I come in and speak with you?" she asked. Phillip opened the door and showed her to a chair.

Mary looked at him solemnly. "I wish to arrange a memorial for my brother, but Abigail is convinced he is still alive. She will not grieve or even acknowledge that we are in mourning. When I try to talk to her about it, she answers that you told her that letter may have come by mistake."

Phillip sighed. "She asked if it was possible, and I told her yes. I didn't know what else to tell her right then."

A faint look of hope crossed Mary's face. "Please tell me the absolute truth, Mr. Valenti. Could this all be a misunderstanding, and my brother be alive and well?"

"I was with him on that day, Mrs. Hamilton," Phillip answered emotionally.

Mary held her breath. "And?" she asked.

Phillip clenched his jaw while tears filled his eyes and he shook his head. "He's gone."

Mary nodded and looked down at her lap. "Mr. Valenti, I'm sorry to have to ask you to do this, but Abigail desperately needs to hear you say these words. She won't listen to me or Clara or Sam, but she will believe you. Please come to the house and tell her."

Phillip followed Mary back to the house where Mary led him to Abigail's room. "Abigail, Mr. Valenti would like to speak to you."

Abigail smiled when she saw Phillip. "You are looking well, Phillip. How is your leg?"

Mary gave Phillip a pleading look before she turned around and left down the hallway. Phillip stood inside the doorway to Abigail's room. "The leg is getting better every day," he told her. "I expect it will be as good as new soon enough."

"I am glad for you," Abigail replied. "Did you wish to see me about something?"

Phillip took a deep breath and sat on a chair near the door. "I've never told you about that day. The day I got this injury."

Abigail looked at him compassionately. "You did tell me the night you had the whiskey. You said that Ethan saved you from the Germans."

"Yes…yes that's true…" he said. "It was bad, Abigail. The only reason I'm alive today is because he pulled me out. But then…then he had to go back in. It would be a miracle for anyone to survive that battlefield. It was the fifth day of September."

Abigail's chin began to tremble. "Do you believe he died that day?" Phillip nodded. Abigail looked down at the quilt on her lap. "I see." Tears began to fall and Phillip handed her a handkerchief from the top of the bedside table. She then asked emotionally, "Will you come to my husband's memorial service?"

"I'll be there," he replied, choking the words out. Phillip quietly left the room and met Mary and Clara on the upstairs landing. "She'll have the memorial service."

Mary and Clara breathed in relief. "Thank you, Mr. Valenti," Mary said sincerely. "This means the world to my family and me."

"I think you should know his last words on that day," Phillip told her. "He made me swear to take care of you and Abigail. You were on his heart until the very end. If there's anything you ever need, I'm here for you."

Mary hugged Phillip, her tears falling on his shoulder as she whimpered, "Thank you."

Abigail remained alone in her room, gazing mournfully at the small wooden carving that she held. She knew in her heart that she could not bear to spend the holidays at Davenport House...knowing that her husband was never coming back.

PART II

In the seasons that followed, the world faced a new crisis that proved worse than the War. An outbreak of Spanish Flu, together with the shortage of medical staff, was felt dreadfully by all. Many ladies on the home front were compelled to join the Red Cross in an effort to preserve what was left of the nation. It was with the Red Cross that Abigail found escape from her grief for many months...but a timely letter from Mary was enough to persuade her that a noble cause awaited her back at Davenport House...

CHAPTER 8

Spring of 1918, Davenport House

"This is going to be a grand party, I see," Mary said to Clara while admiring the decorations in the Hall.

"I was born to plan parties," Clara stated with confidence. "It is also how I make up for not having the big wedding I always wanted."

"I'm sorry about that, Clara. Any idea of when Lawrence will be home?"

Clara shrugged. "He is still with his mother. I've offered to travel to Pittsburgh so that I can help too, but he insists it is too dangerous right now."

"He may be right about that. The outbreak is worse than I have ever seen it. William said there are not enough undertakers in the country to keep up, and he has forbidden any pregnant women from entering the clinic."

"The county is fortunate to have a capable midwife now," Clara said.

Mary smiled. "I suppose I began just in time. I can hardly keep up with the births. I'm only glad that Abigail is returning tomorrow. I need all the help I can get!"

"I wonder how she is doing," Clara said quietly. "None of us expected her to leave so soon after Ethan's service."

"Her letters sound cheerful enough. I think it has done her well to be away and feel useful," Mary replied. "Staying busy is all that keeps my mind off how grieved I am for my brother. When I go to bed at night, all the tears that I hold back during the day suddenly come out."

Clara put her hand on Mary's shoulder. "I'm sorry that William cannot be here now. We can only pray for the end of this terrible outbreak so we may move forward with our lives."

Sam was in the stable tending the horses when Fiona arrived breathlessly. "There is a letter in the post for you today," she said, handing him the envelope. "I can read it with you tonight, but I have to get back to the house now. Miss Clara is planning a great party for your sister's homecoming."

Sam grinned as she scurried away. "Thank you, Fiona. Good luck with the party!"

Late that night after everyone had gone to bed, Fiona heard a soft knock at her bedroom door. She climbed out of bed and turned on the bedside lamp, then opened her door a little ways. "Sam? What are you doing here?" she whispered.

"I'm sorry to bother you, but I never got to hear what the letter says," he whispered back.

"I got so busy today that I forgot about it," Fiona replied. "I'll get dressed and meet you in the kitchen."

Sam was nervously pacing in the kitchen when Fiona came to him. "I know I shouldn't be here at this time of night, but I got scared. It doesn't look like Jenny's other letters."

Fiona took the letter from Sam and noticed that it was not Jenny's handwriting. "You're right, it doesn't look like the others," she said, carefully opening the envelope. Her heart sank when she saw the enclosed lock of hair and the words that accompanied it. "Sam…it is from Jenny's father." He nodded sadly and waited for her to read.

Samuel,

Our hearts are heavy, for influenza has entered our home and taken Jenny to be with our Lord. She asked us to send this lock of hair for you to remember her by. Our family looks forward to the day when we can all be together again in Heaven. I'm sorry, Son.

Gary

Fiona gave it back to Sam. "I'm terribly sorry," she said quietly.

"It's my fault," Sam muttered. "It shouldn't have taken me so long to get our house built. If I'd just worked harder…she would be here with me now…"

"It could never have been your fault," Fiona responded.

Sam buried his head in his hands. "Why did I take so long? If only I hadn't—" his words were muffled between cries. Fiona went to the cupboard to get a glass of water for Sam, but when she turned around, he was no longer there. Fiona poured the water into the sink and returned the glass to the cupboard before going back to bed. She silently lay in bed looking up at the ceiling while tears rolled down the sides of her face.

The next morning, Phillip drove Clara to the train station to meet Abigail. "I wonder if she'll even recognize us in these ghastly things," Clara remarked, referring to the gauze masks they wore to cover their mouth and nose.

"She'll likely be wearing one too," Phillip replied. "At least, I hope she is." The people in town wore identical gauze masks to prevent the spread of influenza. The ones who had no mask held handkerchiefs to cover their faces.

They arrived at the station just as Abigail was stepping off the train with her traveling case in hand. Clara waved at her. "Abigail! Over here!"

Abigail walked over to hug Clara while Phillip took her traveling case. "Welcome home, dear," Clara greeted.

"Thank you, Clara. I am glad to be coming home." She turned to Phillip. "You look well. Your leg must be healed by now."

"Healed enough to drive again, and that's good enough for me," he answered shyly.

They climbed into the car and soon arrived at Davenport House, where they could finally remove the gauze masks. The house was decorated with streamers, balloons, and colorful flower arrangements. A large banner read:

WELCOME HOME ABIGAIL

Abigail could not help but laugh. "You did not go through all of this trouble just for me," she said.

Clara beamed. "Are you kidding? It was the most fun I've had in ages!"

Mary walked through the front door just then. "Abigail!" she exclaimed, hugging her friend tightly.

"Let us go to the drawing room while we catch up," Clara said. Tea and cakes were set out on a lace tablecloth in the center.

"How did you enjoy worknig with the Red Cross?" Mary asked her.

Abigail managed a smile. "It was rewarding at times, and difficult at other times," she said thoughtfully. "I'm looking forward to delivering babies with you from now on."

"You came just in time. I have five women who are sure to deliver by the end of the week."

"Oh dear, I will do my best," Abigail giggled. "The last time I attended a birth was when my mother delivered my little sister. I don't remember much of it."

"You'll be an expert in no time," Mary assured her. "I lost count of the births I attended after a hundred."

"Oh, let's not talk about work right now," Clara said. "We are going to have a lovely party tonight in honor of Abigail coming home. I asked Mrs. Malone to make your favorite dishes and we will all wear our best dresses."

Before the party started that night, Abigail walked to the Valentis' farmhouse. Phillip answered the door in surprise. "Abigail," he said. "Good evening."

"Good evening, Phillip. I bought these delightful ribbons in Philadelphia for Serena. I thought she might like to wear them to the party tonight."

"Oh—um—I guess you haven't heard. Serena never came back."

"What do you mean? Is she alright?"

"She telephoned the house saying she needed more time in Pittsburgh, and that's when she found out that I had come back home. I guess she decided to stay with Angelina."

Abigail smiled. "That's understandable." She noticed that Phillip was still in his day clothes. "Aren't you coming to my party? Clara intends to make a spectacle of me, you know."

Phillip laughed nervously. "I know, but...I have the children..."

"You must bring them! I am always cheered to see their faces. Please bring them tonight."

"I'll send them over just as soon as I can get them ready."

"Then, you won't be coming too?" Abigail asked in confusion. Phillip hesitated to answer. Abigail sensed awkwardness between them. "What is it? Why don't you want to come?"

Phillip cringed. "It's just that—I started to remember some of the things I said to you the night you were here—I've been embarrassed ever since. I hope you can forgive me."

"Oh—that," Abigail sputtered, beginning to feel embarrassed herself. You need not worry about any of that. It was I who made you drink a full bottle of whiskey. I haven't given it a second thought. Please, say that you will come to the party tonight."

"If you want me to be there, I'll be there," he acquiesced.

In the servants' quarters of the house, Sam asked the cook for a plate of dinner to take back with him to the stable. She looked at him quizzically. "Why aren't you up there for the party? It's for your own sister."

Nora overheard and scoffed. "He must not have been invited. He's been moping around since yesterday. He wouldn't own anything fancy enough to wear up there anyway."

"That's enough, Nora," Fiona scolded. "It's Sam's business whether he attends the party or not. Now take this tray to the banquet table." Nora obeyed and Sam left the kitchen quietly. Fiona noticed that he left before Mrs. Malone could serve up a plate for him.

Upstairs in the library, the telephone began to ring. Mary was called to a birth and had to leave. The next telephone call was for Clara from Lawrence. Clara sat in the library near the phone. "Lawrence, I am still waiting on the money. Haven't you sent it yet?"

"I'm sorry, my dear. I'll send it first thing tomorrow," he replied distractedly.

Clara breathed in frustration. "You've been saying that since last year. I'm losing hope." The other end was quiet. "Lawrence, if you spent the money, then just say so. I think it's lovely that you bought me jewelry, but I already have more than enough necklaces."

"What jewelry are you talking about?"

Clara heaved a sigh. "I saw the diamond necklace in the bureau. I know it must have been terribly expensive. Why don't you just sell the necklace and send me the money."

"Oh—that necklace. I'm sorry, my dear, but I did not buy it for you. It was for my mother. She never got to have nice things, you know, so I wished her to have it. She's wearing it as we speak. I can't ask for it back now."

"No, I suppose you can't," Clara groaned. "Will you be coming home soon?"

"I'll be there before you know it, Clara. Goodbye, my dear." Clara hung up the phone in disappointment. Fiona was standing near the doorway of the library and had overheard every word.

In the drawing room, the Valenti children were asking Abigail many questions. Phillip finally intervened. "Gabriella, Donnie, that's enough questions for Miss Abigail in one night. Why don't you go and have some cake."

"Hooray!" the children said in unison, and scrambled to the banquet table.

Abigail laughed. "Thank you for bringing the children. They have made this party the perfect homecoming for me."

Phillip pulled up a chair next to her. "I heard that you returned to assist Mary in midwifery," he said.

"I did. Mary had to leave tonight but insisted that I stay for my party. I am nervous about the first time I will be present to deliver a child," she told him. "I have butterflies every time I think of it."

Phillip chuckled. "It's not hard at all. If I can do it, you can too."

Abigail looked at him with wide eyes. "You've helped with a birth before?"

Phillip laughed again. "Who do you think delivered Gabriella and Donnie?"

"I did not realize."

"Sofia had them so fast, there was never time to wait for a midwife. Gabriella came out nice and easy. But Donnie… he was the one who gave us a scare."

"What happened?"

"When Donnie came out, the cord was wrapped around his neck real tight. He turned blue," Phillip shuddered to remember it.

"What did you do?"

"I unwrapped the cord and breathed into his mouth. It happened so fast, but it was instinct. I just had to get him to breathe again."

"Goodness. Well, you have done a fine job with Donnie. He is healthy and happy now."

Clara walked into the room just then. "I'm sorry I had to desert you for the telephone call, Abigail."

"It's alright, Clara. Thank you for having this lovely party for me. I am having a good time."

"It is my pleasure," replied Clara. She looked toward the banquet table. "Oh dear, the children have already gotten a piece of cake! I was too late to serve it properly. Goodness, they do not even have a plate!" Abigail and Phillip laughed as they watched the children joyfully eat the cake they held in their hands.

Later that night, Fiona went to the stable and knocked on the door to the apartment above. Sam opened the door and looked at his feet sadly. "I don't think I can talk right now, Fiona."

"I didn't come to talk, only I noticed you never took a helping of dinner from Mrs. Malone. I brought some leftovers from the banquet tonight, and some cake, if you would like it." Fiona held out a tin for Sam.

"I am grateful," he said, taking the tin from her.

"Goodnight, Sam."

"Goodnight."

Chapter 9

The following day, Clara summoned Fiona to meet her in the library. "Close the door behind you, Fiona," she told her solemnly.

"What did you need to see me about, Miss Clara?" she asked.

"The reason I called you in is because one of the maids has complained about you. It seems quite serious," Clara began.

"Oh?" Fiona said nervously. "I know that Nora does not like me much."

"It was not Nora. It was Jane. That's why I am taking the matter more seriously."

Fiona could feel her heart beating wildly. She could not imagine what Jane could have said to her.

Clara continued, "Did Sam come to your bedroom after everyone had retired for the night?"

Fiona's eyes grew wide. "He did—Miss Clara—but it wasn't like that!" she stammered.

"What happened?"

Fiona took a deep breath while she tried to think of

how she would answer. "You see, no one really knows except Miss Abigail, but Sam never learned to read. I've been reading him the letters that his fiance sends him from Johnstown."

"I see. It does not seem a good reason for him to be visiting you in the middle of the night, though," Clara replied.

"It only happened that one night because it was an emergency. I meant to read the letter earlier in the day, but became busy and forgot. Sam observed that the note was not written in her hand, and he worried it might be bad news."

"Was it?"

Fiona nodded. "She has died of influenza, Miss Clara."

"How terrible. I had no idea Sam was engaged," Clara said.

"He keeps these things to himself, Miss Clara. I haven't said a word of this to anyone except for you just now."

"I knew there would be a reasonable explanation. I was going to speak with Sam after meeting with you today, but I no longer think it is necessary. However, you will need to give Jane an explanation. She should not have to worry about men coming into the servants' quarters at night."

"Yes, Miss Clara. I'll be sure to get it sorted with her."

"Very good. Thank you for telling me the truth. I would rather that everyone is honest with me than forcing me to guess whether or not they can be trusted."

Fiona held her breath while a sinking feeling washed over her. She remained there awkwardly, staring at Clara as if the words would burst forth at any moment. Clara looked at her curiously. "What is it?"

"Oh Miss Clara, there is something you should know about Mr. Collins, but I don't know how to say it!"

"My husband? What do you mean? Fiona, I beg of you to tell me whatever it is that you know."

Fiona looked at the floor. "Do you remember when my sister left the house? It was because Mr. Collins wanted her to be with him in another room after you had gone to sleep."

Clara's mouth hung open in shock. "I can't believe it!"

"It's true, Miss Clara. Before Mr. Collins ever came here, he knew Bridget in Philadelphia. He made her think that he would marry her. Then he did not contact her for months. When he moved into this house, he told Bridget it was to be with her."

Clara looked down at the desk, feeling as if she would fall to the floor if she did not hold on for support. "Now I wish that you never told me any of this. I know I said that I wanted the truth, but…how humiliating. Are you certain about this, Fiona? How do you know your sister didn't make it up?"

Fiona approached the desk and reached into her apron pocket. "He gave her this," she said quietly, laying the diamond necklace on the desk. "Bridget wanted to return it to you, but did not know how. I have been trying to find the proper way to get it back to you."

Clara looked at the necklace in horror. "Did she—did they—stay in another room—after Lawrence was married to me?"

"No, Miss Clara," Fiona said quickly. "Bridget refused to meet with him and left for the Red Cross the next day."

Clara clenched her jaw emotionally. "I don't wish to hear any more. I need your promise that you will not say a word of this to anyone."

"I promise, Miss Clara." Fiona left the room and Clara

laid her head on the desk in front of her, feeling the stabbing pain of betrayal in her heart.

When Fiona exited the library, she crossed paths with Abigail in the Hall. "Good morning, Fiona. If anyone asks for me, will you tell them I have gone outside to see my brother? I'm going to tease him for not coming to my party last night."

"Um—Miss Abigail—before you talk to Sam," Fiona stammered. "There's something you should know. He has learned that Jenny passed away. He received the news from her father the night before you returned."

Abigail put her hand to her heart in sorrow. "Oh no… dearest Jenny…Sam must be devastated. Thank you for telling me, Fiona."

Fiona nodded and went down to the servants' quarters, heading for her room as quickly as she could. She was weary of the secrets she carried and the pain of telling those who were affected. As she rounded the corner to her bedroom, Nora stopped her in the hallway. "So, did you get into trouble?"

"I don't wish to be bothered," she said, pushing her way past Nora and into her bedroom. She closed the door and sank down to the floor, hoping and praying that she had done the right thing.

At the stable, Abigail found Sam on a bale of hay, staring blankly in front of him. "Welcome back, Abby," he told her stoically.

Abigail sat down next to him. "I'm terribly sorry about Jenny."

Sam nodded. "I feel like I'm out of my mind. I don't know how you manage every day after losing your husband."

"I don't know how either, Sam." She paused for several moments while she thought about it. "Perhaps it made a difference that I began mourning for him the day he left for the War. When I received the news that he wasn't coming back, it was as if I was still in mourning—but it was a new grief that came with certainty. In a strange way, it was easier to know for sure about him than to be in a constant state of worry."

"I forgot to water the horses yesterday. I'm worried what else I might forget when I'm messed up like this," Sam told her. "I even forget to eat, then my stomach makes noises all night."

Abigail laid her head on his shoulder. "I understand. I will do my best to take care of you—"

They were interrupted by Mary bursting into the stable. "Abigail! It's time! Are you ready to attend a birth?"

"Yes, I'll be right there, Mary," Abigail replied, giving Sam an apologetic look. She kissed him on the cheek and followed Mary out to the car where Phillip was waiting for them.

When they arrived at their destination, the ladies worked quickly to ensure a safe delivery. It was not long before the mother held the new baby girl in her arms. Mary sent her medical kit with Abigail to take back to the car while Mary spoke to the new mother about what to expect next.

"That was fast," Phillip remarked. "How did you enjoy your first time attending with Mary?"

Abigail managed a smile as Phillip helped her climb into the car. "It was not as difficult as I expected, but also quite tiring."

"Yes, of course," Phillip chuckled. He noticed that

Abigail was looking sorrowfully into the distance. "Abigail," he said softly, "You know I care for you a great deal. You have helped me more than I can ever repay in one lifetime. If there is anything you need or anything I can do, just say the word."

She turned her head to meet his gaze. "There is something you can do…if it's not too much trouble."

"Anything."

"My brother has just received some dreadful news from home. It will take him time to recover, and in the meantime, well—if you could just check with him for any help he might need—help with the horses, that sort of thing."

"Of course I will," he told her sincerely.

Mary came out to the car and heaved a sigh of relief. "We'll return to check on the mother in a few days. What did you think, Abigail?"

"You did a lovely job, Mary. I have new admiration for you, now that I know this is what you do every day. It was exhausting!"

Mary laughed. "It sure is. Now you see why I'm eager for your help!"

When Mary and Abigail returned to Davenport House, Fiona met them in the Hall. "Post for you, Miss Abigail," she announced.

Abigail opened the letter and frowned in disappointment. "Oh no, Mary. Come read this—it concerns you too."

Mary read the letter in sadness. "Those poor people. This means we will have no income," she whispered. "We may have to move into the manor house."

"What is it?" asked Clara, who had just come down the stairs. "Not more bad news…"

"It is bad news, I'm afraid. The tenants of the manor

house and all of the servants have passed of influenza. Only the housekeeper survived and wrote to inform us."

Clara reacted angrily. "Will there be no end to this grief? It's as if the whole world is ending! Did you know the town hall is being used to store the bodies? This influenza is from hell itself."

Mary was quiet. Abigail broke the silence, "Clara, this means that Mary and I have lost our income from the manor house. We won't have the means to pay you as much in rent until we have new tenants at the house. It may be difficult to find anyone who wants it after what happened. Or we could move there ourselves and—"

Clara broke out into tears. "Please don't leave me," she cried. "Not now. I don't want to be alone here."

Clara's sudden reaction surprised them. Mary put her arm around her. "We won't make any decisions just now, Clara. But we cannot stay and be a burden on you either."

"I want you to stay," Clara told them. "Both of you. I don't care about the money. Honest."

Abigail could not help but feel sorry for her. "If you are certain, Clara. We don't wish to take advantage."

"It won't be taking advantage if I am pleading with you to stay," she assured them. "Please say you will."

"You are too generous," Abigail told her. "Thank you."

"Yes, thank you, Clara. We will stay," agreed Mary.

After dinner that night, Mary visited Abigail in her bedroom. "I wanted to check on you, to see how you are feeling after today. I know that attending a birth can bring out many emotions."

Abigail closed the bedroom door. "It was dreadful for me, Mary," she admitted. "Not because of the sights or the other difficulties…but because it made me realize that I will never be a mother."

Mary sighed. "I'm sorry…I didn't think of that."

"You and William are sure to have children soon, and even Clara will when Lawrence returns. But I will not have that chance again. I always hoped I would have many children."

"You are only twenty, dear. You have time to marry again, if it is what you wish to do," Mary said gently.

"I didn't expect you to suggest that I could remarry. I was afraid that if I spoke of it, I may give the impression that I did not love Ethan so much after all."

"No one could believe you did not love him," replied Mary. "Have you—thought of marrying again?"

"Sometimes I think that I could," she admitted. "But other times, I think that Ethan might walk through the door at any moment, proving that the last year was only a bad dream."

Mary smiled. "I understand that hopefulness. But we also must be real. I want to see you happy, and if it means marrying another man and having a large family, then I hope that's what you will do."

"Thank you, Mary," Abigail said timidly.

"Goodnight, Abigail."

"Goodnight."

Later that week, Abigail went to the stable to check on Sam. She was surprised to find Donnie and Gabriella sitting on the haystacks there. "Good morning," she greeted them.

"Good morning, Miss Abigail," Gabriella replied. "Papa is helping the man who works here. He said we could stay in the stable as long as we did not get into mischief."

"I see," Abigail replied. "How long have you been here?"

"A hundred hours," Donnie replied in an exasperated tone.

"More like five hundred hours," Gabriella corrected him.

Abigail smiled and sat on the haystack next to Donnie. He cuddled up to her arm and looked dreamily into her eyes. "Miss Abigail, you are *bellissima*."

Abigail giggled. "What does *bellissima* mean?"

"It's what our papa calls you," explained Gabriella. "He says you're the most *bellissima* lady in America." Donnie nodded in agreement.

"Then I will have to ask your papa what it means," Abigail replied playfully. Phillip and Sam walked into the stable just then.

"Hello Abby," Sam greeted her before turning to shake hands with Phillip. "Thank you again, Mr. Valenti."

"Papa, are you done yet?" Donnie moaned. "We've been waiting five hundred years."

"Five hundred years! No wonder I feel like an old man," he said to Donnie, but he was smiling at Abigail. "How about we go home and have some lunch?"

"I'm so hungry, I could eat a whole chicken," Gabriella said dramatically.

"I could eat two chickens," Donnie retorted. The Valentis walked back to their house leaving Abigail and Sam in the stable.

"Boy, that Valenti fellow sure helped me this week. I'm all caught up now. He just showed up out of the blue and said he had extra time," Sam told her.

"That was kind of him," Abigail replied.

"He saved my skin, that's for sure. But don't tell Pa I said so. He'd hate it if he knew I was working with an Italian."

Abigail laughed. "I won't tell our pa. But remember, Phillip is an American now. He earned his papers when he fought in the War."

Sam looked at her skeptically. "What's up with you two anyway? Is he just buttering me up so he can ask for your hand?"

"Good grief, Sam. How did you come to that conclusion?"

"I saw how he looked at you…and him showing up to help like this…it all adds up."

"Oh don't tease me, Sam. He's just being neighborly. You should go inside the house now or the maids won't save any lunch for you."

Abigail remained alone in the stable after Sam went into the house. She was not expecting to see Phillip return so soon.

He walked in, shaking his head with a chuckle. "Gabriella left her doll here. I thought I better come back and find it or there will be no peace in our home."

Abigail joined in the search. "The children were sitting just here when I came in, so perhaps the doll is not too far." They began to look around and behind the haystacks. Finally, Abigail found the doll laying on the ground, covered with hay. "She must have been putting the baby to bed," Abigail remarked as she dusted off the doll and brought it to Phillip.

"Thank you," he sighed. "Now that the important doll is found, the world may stop coming to an end at the farmhouse." But he continued to stand there, gazing at Abigail as if he wanted to say more.

"Phillip…what does *bellissima* mean?"

He smiled bashfully. "Where did you hear that word?"

"From the children."

"Of course."

"Well?" she prodded.

He looked into her eyes. "It is how we say, *most beautiful.*"

Abigail stepped closer to him and put her arms around his neck. She felt his arms around her waist and she laid her head on his chest. "I just wanted to know what it would feel like to be held again," she said quietly, enjoying the feel of his heartbeat against her ear.

"I can do this for as long as you'd like," he replied.

Abigail closed her eyes and listened to his deep breaths. "Phillip…do you love me?" His heart raced against her ear and his breathing abruptly halted. Abigail opened her eyes and looked up into his.

"Yes," he answered. His gaze drifted from her eyes to her lips, but he remained still.

Abigail finally leaned into him and pressed her lips to his, forgetting everything else that may have kept her from doing so. They held each other tightly until they heard little footsteps running toward the stable.

"Papa, did you find her?" Gabriella called breathlessly. "Did you find my dollie?"

Phillip was jolted back to reality and he and Abigail backed away from each other. "Gabriella, you are supposed to be helping Donnie with his lunch."

"We've already had lunch," she replied. "I need my dollie."

Phillip gave her the doll. "Now go back home and I'll be along shortly."

Gabriella hugged her doll tightly and skipped out of the stable. Phillip shook his head. "Sorry about that. The children seem to interrupt at the worst times."

"I should be getting back to the house anyway," Abigail said, looking at the floor.

"When will I see you again?" asked Phillip.

Abigail looked up to meet his gaze. "I feel terribly guilty for what I just did. I am sorry." Abigail hurried away from the stable. When she got into the house, she nearly ran into Mary in the Hall. "Oh, I'm sorry, Mary."

"I'm going to a birth," Mary explained, holding her kit.

"I'll change my clothes and be right down," Abigail told her.

"Wait, Abigail—" Mary stopped her. "I wonder if you could stay here. Clara has been awfully quiet and I'm worried about her. She won't tell me what's wrong but perhaps she'll talk to you. She is in the sitting room upstairs."

"I'll go to her. Good luck, Mary."

When Abigail arrived in the sitting room, Clara was staring blankly at the fireplace. "Good afternoon, Clara," Abigail greeted.

"Good afternoon," she replied quietly.

"I have just asked for Fiona to bring us tea," Abigail said, taking her seat in the chaise lounge.

Clara looked at Abigail. "Have you heard from Bridget recently?"

"She telephoned just this morning about the manor house. She said the Red Cross is asking to use it as an emergency hospital since it is sitting vacant now. And of course I saw Bridget every day in Philadelphia," Abigail replied. "We worked in the same part of the hospital camp."

"Then she really did volunteer for the Red Cross," Clara thought aloud.

"Well yes, why would you think differently?"

"I was worried that she might have been away with Lawrence all this while."

Abigail looked bewildered. "Why would she be with Lawrence?"

"Did you know that they were sweethearts before he came to live here?"

Abigail was aghast. "What? Clara, I had no idea of anything like this. Where did you hear it from?"

"As if it wasn't bad enough to have a husband who humiliates me, I had to learn about their attachment from my own housekeeper. Fiona said that Bridget knew Lawrence from when she was your maid at the manor house."

Abigail's eyes were wide. "The only attachment I was aware of was the one Bridget seemed to have the postman. It couldn't have been Lawrence. Isn't he an attorney?"

"It's what he told me. But I don't know that I can believe what he tells me. He never sent the money back, even after he promised repeatedly."

Abigail quietly gasped. "Oh dear, Clara. I thought that had been sorted long ago."

Clara shook her head. "I thought it was…but he has lied to me since the day we met. I don't know what to do about it. He is not even here for me to confront him."

"I'm terribly sorry. Is there anything I can do for you?"

"There is something you can do. I would do it myself, but I'm rather depressed about it." Clara left the room and returned with the diamond necklace.

"Could you take this to the jeweler in town today? I spoke to him on the telephone and he promised to pay a good price for it."

Abigail took the necklace from Clara. "If there is anything else I may do for you, you need only ask." She prepared to leave for town and asked Fiona to summon Sam.

"Sam has taken Miss Mary to her appointment," Fiona answered. "I will go tell Mr. Valenti that you need a driver."

"It's alright, Fiona. I will tell him myself."

Phillip was pleased to see Abigail arrive at his home. "The children are sleeping," he told her. "Please come in."

She walked into the farmhouse but did not sit down. "Actually, I did not come to visit. I was hoping you could drive me into town in Clara's car. I have to meet with the jeweler."

"Of course. I will just leave a note for Gabriella," he told her. "She is fine to care for Donnie as long as we are not away for long." Abigail watched him write a note and leave it on the kitchen table.

"You are a good father," she remarked.

Phillip smiled. "I love my children…I would be glad to have more, if I ever had the chance."

"I would too."

"Do you still feel guilty about what happened today?" he asked.

"I don't know what I feel. I'm confused—and terribly lonely."

Phillip stepped closer to Abigail and slid his hands around her waist. "You don't have to be. I would do anything to make you happy."

"I believe you would," she said, relaxing into his arms.

"Will you let me?"

"I—I—" she stammered. "I need to speak with my brother first. I need to know that he will understand."

Phillip kissed her hair. "I hope he does, Abigail. It would make me very happy."

"Oh dear, we really must get to town before the jeweler closes up shop," Abigail told him. "We can talk more on the way there."

When Abigail returned to the house after visiting the jeweler, she gave Clara the cash from the sale of the necklace. Clara was grateful to receive it and hid the money in a safe place. Abigail went to the stable apartment to see her brother before dinner.

"Sam, there is something I must speak to you about," she told him.

"Would it have anything to do with you and the Valenti fellow kissing in the stable?"

Abigail gasped. "You saw that?"

Sam laughed. "I just shook my head and left before I lost my lunch."

Abigail covered her face with her hands. "Oh come on, Sam. I'm already embarrassed. And yes, I do wish to speak to you about Phillip. I think I would like to be with him, only I wanted to hear what you had to say about it."

Sam shrugged his shoulders. "He isn't Irish."

"Neither was Ethan," she said.

"Do what makes you happy, Abby. None of us knows how much time we have left," he said, pausing in sorrow. "I wish I wouldn't have waited so long to be with Jenny. Now it's too late for us."

"How are you managing with it?"

He shrugged again. "Just trying to get through each day."

"I understand," she told him. "Then, you would be alright if I married Phillip? You would gain a darling niece and nephew."

"I don't mind as long as he is good to you. Abby, if

you're sure that you want to be with him, take my advice and don't wait."

Abigail hugged her brother gratefully. "Thank you, Sam." She returned to the house and saw Mary on the upstairs landing. "Mary, you're home. How was it?"

"Perhaps I should have taken you with me after all," Mary answered. "It started out difficult, but we managed in the end. Mother and baby are both well."

"I'm glad to hear it. Would you come talk to me in my room while I dress for dinner?"

"Yes, but we should hurry," Mary laughed. "I'm starving."

Abigail changed her clothes behind the room divider while Mary sat on the bed. "Did you find out what was bothering Clara?"

"She is having trouble with Lawrence. We should do everything we can to help her," Abigail replied.

"Oh, what a shame she is having trouble with him. I know I miss William desperately. It is hard to not see him for months like this. He said that he may come home in a week to have a rest."

"I hope he does, Mary. I know you miss him dearly." Abigail stepped out from behind the room divider. "There is more I want to say to you before we go down for dinner. Bridget telephoned today and asked if the manor house could be used as an emergency hospital for the Red Cross. They are overfull at the hospital in Philadelphia and need to move the camps indoors."

"I see. We are not living there anyway. It seems a good use of the house," Mary said. "What do you think?"

"I'd be glad to answer that they can use the manor house, with your permission."

"Yes," smiled Mary. "Let us answer them right away. Is that all you wished to speak about?"

Abigail took a deep breath. "There is something else. I think that after dinner tonight…I would like to move into the farmhouse…with Phillip…as his wife." Mary stared with wide eyes and Abigail regretted that she had said anything. "After what you said the other night, I thought you understood."

"I'm only surprised. I did not realize it could be so soon."

"Is it too soon?" Abigail's countenance fell. "I'm sorry, Mary."

"Do you love him?" Mary questioned.

"I feel like I do. When he embraced me today, I felt safe and cared for. I had forgotten what that was like."

"I'm sorry for my reaction. I was not expecting you to marry again just now, but if it makes you feel cared for and safe…then I believe it is what you should do."

"Thank you, Mary," Abigail sighed in relief. "I have no idea how Clara might react to this news. Especially when I tell her we do not wish to have a big wedding."

"How will you be married?"

"On the drive back from town today, we agreed that we would be married in the way of the common law, as I was with Ethan."

Mary smiled and hugged Abigail. "I will miss you, dear sister, but I do wish for you to be happy more than anything. Let us go down to dinner now and tell Clara. Not only that, I must finally get something to eat before I starve!" When they arrived at the dining table, Abigail shyly told Clara the news.

Clara seemed more than receptive to the idea. "Good

for you, dear," she answered. "Now go and have lots of babies so it may feel as if the world has life in it again."

"Thank you, Clara. It is my hope to have more children as well." Abigail left with her traveling case just after dinner. When she approached the front door of the farmhouse, she could hear that the children were still awake. She knocked quietly on the door.

Phillip was glad to see Abigail with her traveling case. He welcomed her inside and the children looked at her quizzically. "Are you going to stay with us again, Miss Abigail? Is Papa going back to France?"

Phillip whispered to Abigail. "What should I tell them?"

"Say that we will live together as a family," she answered.

Phillip beamed. "Miss Abigail is part of our family now."

Gabriella jumped up and down and clapped her hands. "Is she our new mother?"

Abigail felt her face turning pink. "You may call me Mother, if you'd like."

Gabriella and Donnie rushed to hug her. "I love you, Mother," Donnie cooed.

Abigail was beginning to get emotional. She steadied herself on a chair in the sitting room while the children tried to sit in her lap.

"Now that you have heard our happy news, it is time for bed," Phillip announced to the children.

"Can our mother to put us to bed?" Gabriella asked.

Abigail smiled and gladly obliged, and the children soon drifted to sleep in their room after the long day. When Abigail returned to the kitchen area, Phillip was frantically tidying the room. "Sorry it's a mess," he apologized. "I didn't think anyone was coming tonight."

"I hope it's alright that I did."

Phillip stopped his cleaning and held Abigail close. "I am nervous and happy, and I don't know what to do."

"Why don't we sit and talk?"

They sat together on the sofa. "What would you like to talk about?" asked Phillip, raising her hand to his lips.

"I wanted to tell you that I am half-owner a grand house in Philadelphia. Mary owns it with me. Because the house is vacant at this time, we will allow the Red Cross to use it for a temporary hospital."

"That's very good of you," Phillip replied.

"After the outbreak is over, perhaps you might like to see the manor house. If you like it, we could stay there. Or if you wish to stay here at the farmhouse, we could rent the manor house as before and have an income."

"I see," he answered. "I suppose we have plenty of time to decide."

Abigail giggled nervously. "I suppose we do." In the silence that followed, Abigail laid her head on his shoulder and felt her eyelids growing heavy.

"Are you ready for sleep?" he asked her.

Abigail sat up straight. "Phillip, I wonder if I might stay in the children's room tonight. It may help me to feel more settled in the house."

"If it is what you wish," he replied. "I will be sleeping just down the hall."

Abigail nodded. She opened the door to the children's room and smiled when she observed them sound asleep on the bed. She then went to the washroom to change into her nightclothes. Phillip was standing in the hallway when she came out. She smiled shyly at him. "Goodnight," Abigail said.

"May I kiss you goodnight?" he asked quietly.

Abigail stepped closer to Phillip and put her arms around him. When he leaned in to kiss her goodnight, Abigail forgot whatever plans she had to be apart from him.

In the days that followed, Abigail took the children on walks through the Davenport gardens and to the stable every day to see her brother. It seemed to cheer Sam that the children would come to look at the horses and ask many questions. Abigail delighted in seeing him look well after the sorrowful news he had about Jenny.

One afternoon, Abigail and Gabriella were sitting in the grass by the apple trees behind the farmhouse. Phillip showed Donnie the blossoms on the trees while Abigail styled Gabriella's hair with flowers from the garden. She looked up to see Phillip bowing in front of her with a flower. "*Mi amore*," he said dramatically. The girls laughed, which encouraged Donnie to copy his father and also present a flower to Abigail.

"*Mi amore*," Donnie said. Abigail took him into her lap and hugged him tight.

"Phillip," she finally said. "I must go to Davenport House to see if that paper from the Red Cross has arrived. I would also like to say good afternoon to Mary and Clara."

"As you wish, my dear. We'll have lunch when you return."

When Abigail approached the house, she was delighted to see William's car in the driveway. She hurried to the drawing room where he and Mary were having tea. "William!" she cried when she entered the room. "How lovely to see you again!"

William stood up to greet her. Abigail noticed that he looked aged and had dark circles under his eyes, but

William was cheerful just the same. "I understand that congratulations are in order, Mrs. Valenti."

Abigail giggled. "We decided just last week. How did you ever get away from the clinic?"

"I told them that if I didn't get home to see my wife, I would go mad, and it would be me who needed a doctor. I guess that convinced them."

"Abigail, you and Phillip must come to dinner tonight," Mary said. "It will be wonderful for us to be together again."

"Of course we will come for dinner. I can't stay long just now because we are about to have lunch at the farmhouse. I will see you this evening, Mary. I'm glad you could finally come home, William."

Abigail went into the Hall and greeted Fiona. "Has anything arrived for me in the post?"

"It has just come, Miss Abigail." Fiona gave her the envelope.

William and Mary were walking out of the drawing room when they heard a crash in the Hall. "Dr. Hamilton!" called Fiona.

They rushed to find Abigail on the floor with blood dripping from her forehead. Fiona was kneeled beside her helplessly. "What happened!" cried Mary.

"She fell suddenly and hit her head on the arm of the settee," Fiona explained.

"She's unconscious," William said. He lifted Abigail off the floor and carried her to a fainting couch while Mary held a handkerchief against the wound on Abigail's forehead.

"She does not have a fever," William muttered. "We should quarantine her just in case."

"Perhaps she tripped in the Hall?" Mary offered.

"She didn't trip, Mrs. Hamilton," Fiona stated. "She fainted while reading the post."

Mary followed Fiona back into the Hall and picked up the letter from the floor. "Dear God!" she shouted so loudly that it echoed off the walls.

William came out to see her. Mary's face was pale as she sat on the cold marble floor, her trembling hands still holding the letter. "It is from Ethan—" she sputtered. "He writes that he is coming home—and it is dated two weeks ago!"

CHAPTER 10

Abigail slowly opened her eyes and looked around the room, feeling disoriented. "Have I fallen asleep?" she asked.

Mary, Clara, and William were in the room with her, their expressions grave. Clara finally answered her. "You've had a shock, dear. We all have."

"What do you mean?" she questioned, wincing in pain as she tried to sit up.

"Don't try to get up just now," William told her. He checked her eyes with a flashlight.

"I told Phillip I would be right back for lunch," she said.

"It is past dinnertime now," Mary explained.

"Oh! I can't believe I slept for so long," replied Abigail.

"Do you remember receiving a letter in the post today?" William asked carefully.

Abigail sighed. "Not today. I suppose I dreamed that I had a letter from Ethan, but it is the same dream I've had for months."

"Today...it wasn't a dream dear," Clara said gently.

"Ethan was wrongly declared dead by the war office. He is coming home in a few days."

"That was real?" Abigail buried her face in her hands. "What have I done? Oh no, what have I done?"

William stood up to leave the room. He whispered to Mary, "I am going to bed. Come get me if you need anything." Mary nodded solemnly.

"I must see the letter again," Abigail cried. Mary gave it to her.

> *Abigail,*
>
> *I am writing from the hospital camp in France, but I don't want you to worry for me because I am nearly recovered. I'll be home in three weeks. I can't wait to hold you in my arms again, only this time, I won't let you go.*
>
> *Ethan*

Fiona appeared in the doorway of the room. "Mr. Valenti is here."

"I can't see him," Abigail whimpered. "Clara, will you tell him? I can't go back to the farmhouse tonight."

"I will tell him," Clara promised. She went downstairs to Phillip who waited in the Hall.

"Is Abigail alright?" he asked worriedly. "She said she was coming back a while ago."

"Come sit with me in the drawing room," Clara said, reasoning that it would be better to tell him if he were sitting down.

"Abigail had a letter today—from Ethan. It was written just weeks ago."

Phillip's eyes grew wide. "How is that possible?"

"The army was wrong. Ethan writes that he is coming home this week. Abigail is going to stay here at the house."

Phillip was speechless for several moments. "She wants to stay here?"

"She is in shock," Clara replied gently. "I'm sorry."

Phillip bowed his head in sorrow and left the house before Clara could see him cry.

Mary stayed with Abigail in the bedroom. "How can this be happening, Mary? It is the very news that I longed to hear all of these months, and now that it has come, I feel like I will die. Why could it not have come a week ago? Ethan will never forgive me."

"None of us saw this coming," Mary told her. "I feel that I need to see him with my own eyes before I can believe any of it. How could the army not have told us all this while? I am angry and happy and confused all at once."

"I wish I could be happy, but I am frightened to tell him that I did not wait for him. Reading his words is breaking my heart. He has loved me all along…and even though I loved him…I did not wait like I should have. Oh Mary, this feeling is worse than the grief I felt for him. What will I do?"

"Perhaps we can explain to him once he settles in. If he has spent time at the hospital camp, he may still have injuries to recover from once he arrives. When Ethan sees how much has changed at the house since he left, it may be the best time to explain."

"Am I still married to him?"

"The law will see it that way," Mary answered. "Ethan will have to be told that you moved on."

"But I haven't moved on, Mary!" she cried. "I never would have dreamed of marriage if I thought there was any hope of him returning! He is the man that I loved all this while, and he cannot possibly want me now."

"It is too much to figure out in one night," Mary replied wearily. "The only way we can know anything is when Ethan returns and we can see him for ourselves."

Later that week, Sam drove Mary to the train station to meet Ethan. She did not recognize him at first. His clothes hung off of his body and his hair was beginning to gray. When he saw Mary, he ran to hug and kiss her. "You look well, Mary," he said joyfully. "I know I look like an old man. Hopefully Abigail won't mind too much. Where is she?"

"She's at the house," Mary answered as they made their way to the car. "She worried that she might faint if she came to meet you here." They climbed into the car, and Sam drove them away from the train station.

"Did Valenti ever make it home?" asked Ethan.

"He has been home with his children for months," Mary told him. She was hesitant to say more.

"What's wrong, Mary? I thought you would be happy to see me."

Mary smiled at him and held his hand. "Of course I am overjoyed to see you, dear brother. You must realize that we have all had a shock to find out that you would be coming home. I did not even believe it until I saw you at the station just now."

"Why not? Haven't you been waiting for me all this while?"

"You don't know? The war office informed us that you were killed in the War last September."

Ethan was bewildered. "They did? That's awful. Abigail must have been horrified to hear such a thing. But she discovered it was a mistake as soon as she received the letters from me."

"Ethan," Mary said solemnly. "All of us thought you were dead until just days ago."

"Oh," he mumbled, trying to let the news sink in. "Is Abigail alright?"

"You must be careful with her, brother. She has been fragile since she discovered that you were alive and coming home."

"Of course," Ethan replied. "She must have never received my letters then. I feel badly for her."

When they arrived at the house, Ethan went straight to Abigail's room where she lay in bed with the lights turned off. The glow from the fireplace was all that illuminated the darkness. Abigail heard his footsteps approaching the door. Her heartbeat quickened with each step and she held her breath until she could see him in the doorway. "Abigail?" he said quietly. "Are you in here?"

"I'm in bed," she replied.

He walked toward the bedside table and turned on the lamp. "I can't see you in the dark."

She sat up in bed and faced him mournfully, tears beginning to run down her face. Ethan hugged her to his chest. "I'm here," he whispered. "I'm sorry that you were worried about me. I will never leave you again. I love you more than anything."

Abigail continued to cry into shoulder. She cried harder when she felt how thin he had become.

Fiona walked into the room with a tray of dinner just then. She set it on the table and smiled kindly at Ethan and Abigail. "Welcome home, Mr. Ethan."

Abigail watched as Ethan scooped the food from the plate with his hands and stuffed it into his mouth. He wiped his face with his shirt sleeve and then realized Abigail was watching him. "I'm sorry. I suppose that wasn't very proper."

"We can ask the maids to send up another tray," she said quietly.

Ethan nodded. "I could probably eat ten of those helpings. I'll try to eat the next one slower." The maids brought more food and Ethan ate it heartily. He then lay on the bed next to Abigail and fell asleep. She slipped out of the room to find Mary.

"Mary, I can't," she cried. "I can't tell him. You must tell him for me."

Mary was distressed. "I don't know how I will do it either."

"I'll tell him," Clara said from the doorway. "You two have been through enough."

"Thank you, Clara," Abigail said wearily. Ethan slept all through the night and well into the next morning. The girls were having tea in the drawing room when they heard the front door to the house open and close.

"Fiona," said Clara. "Who just went out?"

"It was Mr. Ethan," she answered.

Abigail gasped. "What if he goes to visit Phillip?" The girls exchanged anxious looks and hoped that Phillip would not be home.

Phillip was stunned when he answered the door. "Valenti!" Ethan greeted. "Good to see you still have both legs."

"Yes—I do—" he sputtered.

"Mary told me the war office reported me dead," Ethan said, shaking his head. "I guess no one knows how to react now that I'm here. That last day I saw you, I thought it would be the last day I saw anyone. I'm only glad we both made it back. Will you come to dinner tonight at the house? I'm sure the girls won't mind."

Phillip would not look him in the eye. "I'm sorry, I can't tonight."

"Then come tomorrow night," Ethan shrugged.

Phillip gave a slight nod. "I'll see what I can do."

When Ethan returned to the house, the girls looked at him expectantly. "I went to see Valenti. I tried to get him to come to dinner, but he was acting strange. I guess he has other plans."

Abigail looked at Clara with pleading eyes. Then Abigail and Mary left the room. Ethan looked after them in confusion. "What's going on?" he asked Clara.

"Ethan, you should sit down," Clara told him. "There is something you need to know."

Clara later went upstairs to Abigail's room. "I told him," she said in a tired voice. "I am going to lie down now."

Abigail nodded while tears stung behind her eyes. "Thank you, Clara. Is he still in the drawing room?"

"He went for a ride."

"Did he say anything?"

Clara shook her head. "He never said a word."

Abigail felt restless while she waited in bed, wondering what Ethan might say when he returned from his ride. She finally left the house and waited in the stable so that she could talk to him the moment he returned. The sound of horse hooves galloping in the distance made her heart race. She sat down on a haystack and held on to the sides for comfort. Ethan soon walked in and put the horse away for the night. He did not see Abigail until he turned around in front of her. She stood up quickly. "Ethan," she breathed. "I'm terribly sorry."

He slowly walked to another place to sit down. "It's my fault, Abigail. I should've listened to you when you said we should go to California. This War has taken everything from us. If you knew how many times I wished I could go back to the time you urged me to leave, before it was too late…I feared all along that I would come back to find out you no longer loved me. My worst fear has come true and I have only myself to blame."

"It isn't true," Abigail said, trembling in her seat. "I love you desperately—more than anything or anyone else in the world."

"How can you? You don't know me anymore," he said emotionally. "You would hate me if you knew the things I did over there. I thought I would come home and everything would be just the same as it was when I left. But everything's different. Clara is married, Mary has a profession, and you—you—" Ethan wept into his hands. "We're all different now."

"Ethan, I have loved you all this while," she told him, standing near and running her hands through his hair. "I would never stop loving you because what you did in the War."

"It was bad," he told her sorrowfully. "Unspeakable things that you will never know about. I deserve to go to Hell, but seeing you with another man is more punishment than I can bear. I'm leaving first thing in the morning."

Abigail began to sob. "Don't leave me again! I will die if you do!"

"Isn't it what you want? So you can be with him?"

"I want for you to have stayed and had children with me, and for none of us to have heard of the War! We can't change anything that happened. But if you can forgive me, and stay with me, I will do anything I can to make you love me again."

"You want me to stay with you?" he asked. "What about Valenti?"

Abigail felt her heart drop into her stomach at the mention of Phillip's name. "You are still my husband," she whimpered. "I will be disgraced if you leave now...even more so than I already am."

"Abigail," he said hopefully, looking into her eyes. "You still want to be with me?"

She nodded while tears streamed down her face. "It is what I've been saying all this while. I never could have thought about marrying again if I knew you were coming back. I was afraid when so many people around us were dying of influenza. I worried I might never have the chance again to have children. Jenny, the girl who was going to be my sister-in-law, she is gone now. The tenants of the manor house and all of the servants are gone. I was afraid to keep waiting, but I know I should have. Please, tell me that you'll forgive me someday."

"There's nothing to forgive, Abigail. You did what you thought you should. I only hope you can forgive me for the things I had to do to come back home."

"We can start over and move to the manor house when the Red Cross is through with it," Abigail told him. "Perhaps, after enough time, we will forget that we ever left."

Ethan hugged her tightly. "I hope that we will." They both cried as they held on to each other, and spent what felt like hours in the stable, feeling the release of grief that they carried with them all year. When the tears finally ran dry, Ethan looked into her eyes and leaned in to kiss her deeply. Abigail began to remember how much she missed the way he held her and kissed her. A long-forgotten feeling of peace settled over her while she held onto Ethan's arm, and they made their way back into the house.

Chapter 11

Clara wandered aimlessly through the gardens behind the house and was startled to hear a voice call her name. "Clara? Uh—I meant to say—Mrs. Collins."

She smiled as Joe Blake approached. "Good morning, Mr. Blake. How have you been?"

"Busy," he laughed. "But I've got some new lambs at the ranch and wondered if you might like to have a look."

"Oh—sure," Clara blurted. She followed him to his property.

Joe pointed beside the barn. "You can see the little ones just over there."

Clara gasped. "Oh, aren't they darling! Are they terribly hard to keep?"

Joe shrugged. "They don't bother me one bit. Do you see one you might like?"

"Oh, the one just beside the flowers is lovely," she smiled.

"I'll be sure to remember which one he is when he goes to slaughter," Joe said casually.

Clara looked at him in horror. "Slaughter?"

"Well yes, I thought you wanted him for your Easter supper. Isn't that why you picked him out?"

Clara put her hand to her heart. "No, it's not why at all! I thought you meant for us to have at the estate—to admire and care for."

Joe laughed again. "I suppose you could have him for that, if you wish. Don't you eat lamb for Easter supper?"

"I suppose we do," Clara admitted. "But never after I've already seen it alive and remarked how darling it is!"

Joe tried not to laugh, but he could not help himself. "I sure miss talking to you, Mrs. Collins."

Clara hesitated. "Why don't you come to the house for Easter dinner? We always have plenty of food."

"I'd be glad to," Joe replied. "I'll tell the cows to stay put this time so I don't miss out on your invitation again."

"Very well, Mr. Blake." Clara began walking away.

"But aren't you going to have roast lamb?" he asked.

She called back over her shoulder, "I'm on my way to tell the cook that we will have anything *but* lamb!"

Inside the house, Abigail slowly woke from a deep sleep. She smiled when she saw Ethan next to her. She watched him sleep, all the while convincing herself that he was truly there with her, and it was not only a dream. She then noticed the sunlight streaming in through the windows. "Oh dear, we must have overslept. It must be noon already!"

Ethan groaned and put his arm around her. "Let's just lay here the rest of the week."

Abigail squirmed from his grasp. "You're holding me too tight," she finally sputtered.

He let go immediately. "I'm sorry. Are you alright?"

"Yes," she giggled nervously. "I just couldn't breathe. I am going to wash up and ask the maids to send food up."

"Good. I'm starving," he laughed.

"Mrs. Malone will fatten you up in no time," said Abigail. "She says you are a fine hero and she has promised to give you extra helpings of everything."

"Then she is my heroine," he said wryly, then looked into her eyes. "But you are my one and only. I am glad we have nowhere to be today."

"I may have to leave to help Mary at any moment," Abigail told him.

"What does Mary need help with?"

Abigail smiled. "I suppose I forgot to tell you that I deliver babies now, with Mary."

Ethan looked impressed. "You do?"

"Yes, I have caught several already. It is the most joyous feeling!"

"You look happy, Abigail."

"It's because you are here with me. And you look just the same as you did when you left. There are some men who must wear masks to hide their wounds. Your face looks just as it ever did, and I love it," she said, kissing his cheek.

"What if I had to cover my face? Do you suppose you would still love me?"

"Of course I would. No matter what you look like on the outside, you are still the same on the inside." Abigail kissed him again and left the room.

Ethan lay down on the bed and muttered, "If only that were true."

Abigail soon returned with a tray of food that Ethan ate heartily. "Now, I must go change, for I am to go with Mary to check on an expecting mother."

Ethan nodded. "I'll see what I can do to help out around the estate. I will manage the horses now that I'm here."

Sam drove Abigail and Mary to the house they had promised to visit that day. When Abigail was going to knock on the door, Mary grabbed her arm to stop her. She pointed to the red ribbon that had been tied on the frame. Abigail felt a sinking feeling and they stopped to put on their gauze masks before they knocked on the door. There was no answer.

"Should we go in?" Abigail questioned.

"I don't know," Mary answered. "Let us look in through the windows." The girls circled the house and looked in through the windows they could reach on their tiptoes.

"Do you see anyone?" Abigail called.

Mary walked toward Abigail and hung her head. "We must leave. Death has come to the house, and it spared no one. I saw them through the window."

Abigail repressed the urge to cry and climbed back into the car with Sam. Everyone was quiet on the drive back to the house.

At the pasture of Davenport Estate, Ethan was leading one of the horses into the stable so he could check its shoes. He was startled to see Donnie standing there. "Hello," Ethan said.

"Who are you?" Donnie asked.

"I'm Ethan and this is my horse, Silver," he replied.

Donnie shook his head. "You must be mistaken. That's my mama's horse. She let me ride on his back before."

"Donnie!" called Phillip's voice, sounding distressed. Phillip walked into the stable and froze when he saw Ethan there.

Donnie looked back and forth between the men who stared at each other in a deafening silence. At last, Phillip turned his gaze to Donnie who stood between them. "I told you not to wander from the house," he scolded.

"But I came to see my Uncle Sam. Why can't I come to the stable?"

Phillip grabbed Donnie's hand and led him out as quickly as he could. As they were leaving, Ethan could hear the boy continue to ask his father questions. "Where is our mother? Why hasn't she come back yet?"

Ethan felt sick to his stomach, and went back into the house to lay in bed.

When Abigail and Mary returned to the house, they were glad to see that William had come home for the night. "How was your appointment?" he asked the girls.

"There was a ribbon on the door when we got there," Mary told him. Then she looked at the floor in sorrow.

"I see," William responded. "I'm sorry you had to see that, Mary."

"Will this plague ever be over?" she asked emotionally.

"It's what all of us are praying for," he replied. He held her close, and the both of them went upstairs.

"Fiona," said Abigail. "Have you seen Ethan?"

"I think he is sleeping again, Miss," she answered.

Abigail peeked into the dark bedroom, and was just about to close the door when she heard Ethan's voice. "I'm not asleep, Abigail."

She then walked into the room and explained what happened at the house visit. Ethan was quiet for a long time. "Are you alright?" Abigail finally asked.

"It was a bad day," he answered vaguely. "Sometimes

I feel guilty for coming back…like I'm ruining things for everyone. Are you sure you still want me?"

"Of course I do. Why are you worried?"

"I'm sorry. I worry about a lot of things. Is dinner ready?"

"Just about," she answered with a smile. They went downstairs to dinner where Ethan took great effort to eat like a gentleman once more.

Late that night, after everyone had retired to bed, Abigail burst into the bedroom where Mary and William slept. "I need help," she cried. "Ethan is shouting at me and I don't understand! I'm afraid!"

William leapt out of bed and hurried to the bedroom with Abigail. He turned on the light switch to find Ethan standing in the room, shouting in a threatening manner. His eyes appeared wild and were staring at an invisible enemy.

"What's happening?" Abigail cried, hiding behind William as Ethan swung his fists through the air.

"Don't watch, Abigail," William told her. She covered her eyes and heard a great thud, but the shouting stopped. When she opened her eyes, she saw Ethan flat on his back on the floor.

"Is he alright?" she whimpered.

William rubbed his fist. "He'll have a headache in the morning. Go sleep with Mary tonight. I'm going to stay in here with him in case he starts again."

"Was it a nightmare?"

"Seems that way. Will you be alright with Mary?"

She nodded weakly and walked back to Mary's room, but could not stop trembling even after she lay down to go to sleep.

The next morning, Ethan woke up disoriented on the

floor. He saw William sitting on a chair nearby. "Where is Abigail?" he asked.

"She stayed with Mary," William answered. "You were shouting and threatening her last night."

"Oh no," he exhaled. "I don't remember anything!"

"I didn't expect you would. But you were shouting threats and I had to punch you out before you hurt Abigail or yourself."

"What did I say?"

"You were saying in German—that you would kill everyone."

Ethan buried his face in his hands. "Abigail must think I'm a savage."

"She was frightened and came to wake me. I think it best that you not sleep in the same room anymore."

"I was hoping that I got better. They said I was threatening the nurses in the hospital camp, and I don't remember a thing. They tied me to the bed and said it was so I didn't hurt anyone. They said I was messed up in the head. I never could believe it before, but if you say that I did it… it must be true. What's happening to me?"

"I thought they would have told you at the hospital. They call it shell shock. I've seen it plenty since the soldiers started returning."

"How do I get rid of it?"

William looked at him helplessly. "I don't know the answer to that, Ethan. It may help to find something that relaxes you. Perhaps if you have a project to work on…but it may be something you have for life."

"How could anyone stay sane out there? I can't imagine hell itself being any worse than where I've been. They starved us and messed with our heads deliberately."

"The military?" William asked.

"No, the Germans. I didn't want to say anything to the girls, but I was captured…stuck in a prison camp for six months. I was able to get through the barbed wire one day, but the others were not so lucky."

"You escaped?"

"All I could think of was getting home to Abigail. Now I've ruined that too. I guess I'll go find her and explain that I can't stay here anymore."

Ethan met her later in the upstairs sitting room. "I'm sorry," he told her. "I'm sorry you had to see me like that."

"Are you alright?" she asked in concern.

"I'm not alright. There's something wrong in my head. I'm afraid that what happened last night might happen again, and that's why I'm going to stay at the horse ranch in Yorktown for a while."

"You're leaving?"

"The ranch is short of stable hands. William agrees that it may do me good to work around horses until I start feeling like myself again. Maybe I won't have the nightmares so much."

"I want you to get better," she told him sincerely. "If you believe that staying at the ranch will help, then I will wait for you."

"I don't know how long it will take, Abigail. What if it takes years, or what if I never get better?"

"Then I will wait for you for years or until the day I die, hoping and praying for you to return to me." Both of them were quiet for a long while. Ethan looked down at the floor and Abigail wrung her hands in worry. She finally spoke again, "Before you go, would you stay for Easter dinner? It would help to spend the holiday with you after having so many holidays with you away."

"I will stay for Easter dinner," he promised.

The dining table was set in splendor. Joe Blake attended dinner as promised. He stifled a smile when Clara announced that the Easter meal would be a rib roast. Ethan held Abigail's hand throughout the meal. Abigail could feel her heart sink every time she remembered that he would be leaving afterward. When the dinner was over, Abigail and Ethan slipped away from the others and said their tearful goodbyes at the front door. Abigail then retreated to her bedroom while Ethan and William drove away from the house. Downstairs in the drawing room, Clara was unaware of Ethan's departure and she remained cheerfully conversing with Joe. He smiled slowly and announced that he wished to give a gift to the hostess, but that she would have to go outside to receive it.

"Where are you taking me?" Clara giggled.

"You'll see," he answered mysteriously. They walked to the stable where Sam was ready with the surprise.

Clara gasped. "Is it the same one I chose that day?"

"The very same one," Joe promised.

She laughed in delight as she petted the lamb's soft wool. "Thank you for sparing him for me, Mr. Blake."

"It was my pleasure. I'm sure he'll be glad to have you as a friend. It was you who saved his life, after all."

Chapter 12

Summer of 1918, Davenport House

"Good morning, Mr. Collins," Fiona quietly greeted Lawrence, while taking his hat and jacket.

"Good morning," he replied. "Where is my lovely wife?"

"In the drawing room, Sir."

Clara was speechless when Lawrence walked through the doorway. He went to her and kissed her on the cheek. "I'm pleased to announce that my mother is on the mend, and I am here to stay. Oh, and here is the money I promised you, darling. I'm sorry it took so long." Lawrence handed her an envelope of nearly five thousand dollars. "Should I take it to the bank, or would you prefer to do so yourself?"

"Lawrence, I am astonished to see you! Why did you not telephone to tell me you were coming?"

"But then it would not have been a surprise," he replied. "Aren't you surprised?"

"Well, yes I am," she laughed nervously. She had rehearsed what she would say to him the next time she saw him face to face, but she was beginning to forget it all.

"I got you a present while I was away." He proudly presented her with a velvet box.

Clara opened it slowly. "It's lovely," she said about the diamond necklace that lay within.

Lawrence removed it from the box and clasped it around her neck. "My darling, I have a confession to make. When you found the necklace that day in the bureau, you were correct in thinking that I bought it for you. However, it went missing the very next morning. I could not find it, and even worried that one of the maids might have taken it. Since I was new here, I did not feel I was in a position to begin pointing the finger."

Clara searched his face skeptically. "You truly bought the necklace for me?"

"Of course I did," he laughed. "It is why I have come home with this one for you as a replacement. I wish for you to know your worth to me."

Clara managed a smile and almost felt her doubts fading away. "Thank you, Lawrence."

"Why don't we take a drive around the countryside, like we used to when we were first married?" he coaxed.

Clara nodded and smiled. "I'd like that."

While Clara was in her room changing her clothes, Fiona announced to Abigail that Gabriella had come to the house to see her. Abigail took a deep breath before meeting her in the Hall. "Good morning, dear," she greeted her softly. Abigail could feel her heart swelling at the sight of her.

"Papa said that you are living here now and me and Donnie should call you Miss Abigail again," Gabriella explained sadly. "Why don't you want to be our mother anymore?"

Abigail felt her throat go dry and she swallowed painfully before answering. "You and Donnie are the dearest children in the world," she responded. "You see, the War made many things difficult to understand. One of those difficult things is that I cannot be your mother any longer, but I will be your friend."

"I liked it more when you were my mother," Gabriella pouted.

"I understand, dear—" Abigail was interrupted by Phillip entering through the open door.

He looked intensely at Abigail. "I'm sorry. I didn't know that she was coming here," he said.

Abigail felt butterflies in her stomach as soon as she saw him. It was the first time she had seen Phillip face to face since the day of the letter. When Abigail spoke, it was barely above a whisper. "She only had a question for me. It's alright."

Phillip turned to Gabriella. "Go back home now and we'll talk about it later." Gabriella obeyed and Phillip and Abigail were left alone in the Hall.

Abigail cleared her throat nervously. "I was explaining to her that although I care dearly for her and Donnie, they must only think of me as their friend from now on."

Phillip nodded. "I heard that Ethan is staying in Yorktown now…"

"Yes."

"Is he coming back?"

"He is coming back, but he has not told us when." She paused when Phillip seemed to look at her expectantly. "I will wait for him—however long it takes."

"I see," Phillip replied, looking away from her. "And are you alright?"

"I've been keeping occupied with helping Mary. Um, Phillip…I never properly told you how sorry I am to have left you and the children."

Phillip looked up into her eyes. "I'm sorry too," he said, and turned to leave the house. "Goodbye, Abigail."

"Goodbye, Phillip."

As she returned up the grand staircase, Clara was on her way down. "Are you going to town today?" questioned Abigail.

"Lawrence is back," Clara grinned. "He has brought the money and explained everything. I suppose it was all a misunderstanding when he left last year. We are going to take a drive through the countryside now."

Abigail smiled. "Then I am glad you were able to get it sorted. Um—Clara—" she stammered. "What was Phillip's reaction—that day you told him about Ethan coming home?"

Clara looked at Abigail compassionately. "He was devastated, dear."

Abigail held back tears. "Thank you, Clara. I only wondered. Have a lovely time on your drive today."

Throughout the county and the nation, the outbreak of influenza seemed to be in decline. William returned to stay at Davenport House and intended to work at the clinic only during the day as he had in the past. On the morning that he moved back into the house, William noticed that Mary was about to leave the bedroom in her riding clothes.

"Are you riding alone today?" he asked.

Mary hesitated. "I was going to ask Abigail…"

"I don't want her riding," he replied sternly.

Mary looked at him quizzically. "I did not want to appear rude in not inviting her."

"She is with child, Mary. She can't be galloping through the fields right now."

Mary was taken aback by his statement. "Has Abigail told you that she is expecting?"

"She has not spoken to me, but I can tell by looking at her. I suppose it's an extra sense that I have. I can tell when a woman is expecting, sometimes before she knows, herself. I thought for certain Abigail would have told you by now."

Mary shook her head sadly. "I suspected she may be pregnant, but she has not said a word of it to me. I wondered if I was imagining things."

"You are not imagining things. But you should talk to her about it, Mary. She may be frightened because of what happened the last time she conceived."

"I will talk to her," Mary said. She went down the hallway to Abigail's room. "Good morning," she greeted.

Abigail was still in her nightclothes. Several dresses were laid out on the bed, and her sewing kit was beside them. "Good morning, Mary."

"I was just going for a ride, and I wanted to see—how you were feeling," Mary said.

"I am well," replied Abigail. "Go on ahead without me. I will be occupied with altering my dresses today."

"Because of the baby?" Mary whispered.

Abigail kept her gaze toward the bed. "I wanted Ethan to be the first to know…but he has not replied to my letters. He has sent me his wages, but there is never a note to accompany them."

"I'm sorry, Abigail. We will take good care of you here," promised Mary. "Perhaps Ethan only needs more time."

"I said that I would be fine with however long it took, but I guess I believed he would be back by now."

Mary put her arm around Abigail. "We all thought he would be. I suppose we must keep waiting for him to be ready."

CHAPTER 13

Fall of 1918, Davenport House

Abigail shook her head sadly. "I don't want my brother to know of this," she told Fiona. "The War has taken enough from us. I won't let it take my brother too. Every day, I expect to see the headline that the War is over at last. Instead they are asking for more of our young men."

Fiona nodded solemnly as she watched Abigail place the daily newspaper into the fireplace. They watched the orange glow as the flames consumed the black and white print.

"Did the post go out today?" Abigail asked suddenly.

"It did, Miss Abigail."

"And my letter to Ethan…it went out in today's post?"

"Yes, I made sure of it," Fiona answered.

"Then I will wait for his reply," Abigail said wearily. She placed her hand on her growing belly. "I don't want him to miss anything."

In the billiard room of the house, Lawrence was discussing the handling of the estate with Clara. "I'm only saying that we can sell the land now and invest the proceeds. The land does us no good just sitting there. We don't need five hundred acres anyway, and the rent you charge the tenants is meager at best."

"We have enough money to live on comfortably. I don't see why we should change anything."

Lawrence rolled his eyes. "There is more money to be made, Clara. We are missing out on it."

Clara crossed her arms over her chest. "Oh, why don't you go back to your mother's house in Pittsburgh. All you've done since you've been here is complain about the finances. I've already told you that the only land I wish to part with is what I have already promised to Sam. I don't want to fight about this anymore."

"Fine. Then don't bother me until you have changed your mind about the estate. I grow tired of trying to convince you."

Clara felt painful tears behind her eyes and she softened her tone. "I grow tired of quarreling this way. I truly wish you to be happy with me, darling. Perhaps, if we had a child, it could help settle whatever differences are between us now." When Lawrence did not answer, Clara continued, "Abigail's baby will come soon. Perhaps once you see what a little one is like, you will wish to have one yourself."

Lawrence looked suddenly cheerful. "That is good news," he said.

Clara smiled hopefully. "You think it is good that Abigail is having the baby?"

"Of course. It means she will pay rent for two boarders instead of one. How much is she paying now?"

Clara clenched her jaw in anger and did not answer.

"Clara, answer me," he demanded. "How much does she pay us?"

"She lost her income from the manor house and does

not always get paid when she works with Mary…the wages from Ethan are a pittance…" Clara trailed off.

"How much, Clara?" he shouted.

Clara glared at him. "She is staying in the house as my friend. She pays nothing."

"You call her your friend? She is only taking advantage of you! Does she expect to stay here with the child for free?"

"Lawrence, it is an arrangement that I made with her. It is not your concern!"

"Did you forget that I am your husband, and this house became mine when you married me? Everything that happens here is indeed my concern!"

"The house belongs to me," Clara fumed. "You are referring to antiquated laws that have no business in the modern world. I would think you should have known such a thing if you are indeed a real lawyer."

"Get out, Clara," he told her angrily. "Don't speak to me again unless you are ready act like a real wife."

Clara stormed out of the billiard room and out of the house. It was what she found herself doing often since Lawrence came home for the summer. She only began to relax as she made her way to the pasture and saw the little lamb waiting for her. "Hello, darling," she cooed. "At least you are always glad to see me. I wish you could stay little and sweet forever."

Sam approached Clara from the pasture. "What can I do for you, Mrs. Collins?"

Clara smiled at him. "Nothing just now. I only wanted to see this little one. How have you been, Sam?"

He shrugged. "Alright, I guess. Just working hard so I can get the property paid for by the spring. Thank you for arranging it so I can buy that parcel. It's just what I wanted."

"You're welcome, Sam," Clara said quietly.

"Uh—if you don't need me for anything just now, I'll get these tools returned to Joe. Have a good day, Mrs. Collins."

Joe seemed surprised when Sam approached his property. "Sam," he grinned. "I didn't think I'd see you this afternoon."

"I promised I'd get these tools back to you today."

"Well, after the news in the paper…" Joe replied.

"I don't read the paper," Sam told him. "What did it say?"

"There's another registration for the Draft. Except this time they lowered the age to eighteen. You might be able to get an exception like me, but there's no telling what they'll do once you sign," Joe explained.

Sam went quiet. "I didn't realize. I guess I'll go home now and figure out what I'm going to do about it."

Later that evening in the servants' quarters, the maids began clearing the plates from the kitchen table. Sam stood up and said to Fiona discreetly, "Can I talk to you outside for a minute?"

"Sure," she answered. "I'll meet you just near the servants' entrance once I finish my duties."

Sam was seated on a large boulder outside the servant's entrance while he waited for Fiona to come out. He looked up when he heard her footsteps on the gravel. "Is everything alright?" she asked.

Sam looked at her seriously. "Did you see the paper today?"

"I did see it," she answered quietly.

"So you know what the law says I have to do."

"Your sister was distressed to discover that they are taking the young men now. She hoped you would never hear of it."

"Were you going to tell me?" he asked.

Fiona looked into his eyes. "I was afraid that you would sign up."

"I don't want to. But the war office has different ideas."

"Please don't go, Sam. It will break Miss Abigail's heart. It would be more than she can bear, especially while Mr. Ethan stays away."

"How is Abby?"

"She is weary," Fiona answered. "She was upset when she read about the new Draft. She said the War has already taken her husband from her, and now she is afraid to lose you too…and with the baby on the way…"

"I could go to jail for refusing. Does she understand that?"

Fiona's eyes filled with tears. "Better to be in jail than never come home at all." She started to cry in front of him.

"You want me to stay, don't you?" he asked.

"Yes," she whispered.

"I won't sign up, Fiona," he decided.

Fiona stopped crying. "Do you mean it?"

"I suppose it isn't very honorable of me to disobey the law, but I don't know that I could be so helpful to their cause anyway. I can't imagine killing another man just because I'm told to."

Fiona hugged him tightly and kissed his cheek. "Can I tell Miss Abigail what you have told me—that you won't sign up? She will be cheered by the news."

"Of course you can tell her. Abby needs to hear something that will make her happy," Sam laughed, "even if it's something I might get in trouble for!"

The following weeks were tense at the house. Lawrence and Clara attended dinner together every night, but behaved as strangers. William moved back into the clinic following an outbreak of influenza that threatened to be worse than the last. The ladies of the house prayed daily for relief to come to the nation, and on the thirtieth day of September, a glimpse of hope appeared at the house.

Clara burst into the upstairs sitting room where Mary and Abigail were having tea. "You'll never believe it! Oh, it is the most wonderful news!" she cried.

"What is it?" giggled Mary. "Tell us already."

Clara laughed. "I still can't believe it myself, but our President has moved for support of the votes for women! We might all be voting in the next election!"

"How wonderful," said Abigail. "Your efforts have finally paid off, Clara. Well done!"

Clara beamed. "This is great news for not only the women of today, but for our daughters and granddaughters! I am going to tell the maids. We will celebrate tonight!" Clara hurried out of the room.

Mary turned to Abigail. "What do you think, Abigail? Would you like to vote?"

But Abigail stared blankly toward the window. "Mary, something is happening. I'm in terrible pain all of a sudden."

"Oh dear. Let's get you to bed." Mary helped Abigail to the bedroom.

"I feel a terrible tightening just here," Abigail groaned. "I'm afraid!" She doubled over and cried out loudly.

"You must relax as much as you can. I am going to get you some water." When Mary returned from the kitchen, Abigail smiled weakly.

"The pain has stopped," she said, struggling to sit up straight. "It was agony for those few minutes. I don't know what happened, but I'm sorry to worry you."

Mary sat next to Abigail on the bed and felt a sense of dread. "I would like to examine you just to be sure."

Abigail agreed, but could soon detect the anguish in Mary's expression. "What is it?"

"It's far too early for the baby to come," she told her solemnly. "But it seems your body may not be strong enough to keep the baby in. You will need to stay in bed for the next several months."

Abigail swallowed the lump in her throat. "Do you think I will lose it?"

"We must hope and pray that does not happen," Mary answered. "But you can no longer be on your feet. It would only make it worse."

"If you say so, Mary," Abigail replied sadly. "But do you think we could move my bed near the window first? I want to be able to see when Ethan returns to the house. Oh dear, and Clara wants to celebrate tonight."

"I will have the maids move the bed. You just rest for now. And don't worry, I will explain to Clara."

The months went by slowly for Abigail, who lay in bed, watching the window and hoping for a sign of Ethan's return. Mary walked into the bedroom one day, smiling and crying at the same time. "Abigail, I have some news. It is very exciting, but you must relax as best you can while I tell it to you."

"Is it about Ethan?" she asked quickly.

"No, dear. I'm sorry," Mary said, reaching out to stroke her hair.

"Oh," Abigail frowned. "What is the news?"

"It is the War," Mary told her emotionally. "Germany has signed a peace agreement, and—the War is finally over!"

Chapter 14

Thanksgiving Day, 1918

"How are you feeling today, Abigail?" Mary asked kindly while she brought a tray of tea to the bedroom.

"I will feel better if Ethan comes today. I begged him to come to the dinner, even though I cannot dine downstairs with you."

"I wish you could," said Mary. "Clara has invited all of the servants to dine with us at the table. She said we have the end of the War to be thankful for and should celebrate together."

Abigail gasped at the sound of a car driving up to the house. She held her breath and looked out the window, then let out a sigh. "Mary, William is here."

"He is? I haven't seen him in ages! Thank goodness he has come today!" She felt guilty when she looked at Abigail. "I'm sorry, dear."

"You don't need to be sorry, Mary. I'm glad for you. I hope William may stay for a night at least."

"I will be back with your Thanksgiving meal when it is ready," she told Abigail, then hurried downstairs to see William. She ran to him and hugged him close.

"Happy Thanksgiving," he whispered in her ear.

Mary had tears of joy. "How wonderful that you have come today. What a surprise!"

"I will have to go right back tomorrow morning, but I couldn't go another day without seeing you," he told her, kissing her face all over. "Let's go in now and see if dinner is ready. I'm famished!"

The maids were giddy over being able to dine with the family. Each wore her Sunday best to the dining room. The table was set elegantly with many rows of silver candlesticks. A buffet was laid out with oyster soup, stuffed turkey, potatoes, rum punch, and seemingly endless assortment of pies. "Take a seat in whichever place you'd like," Clara instructed everyone cheerfully.

"It's a splendid dinner, Clara. You have outdone yourself," Lawrence said kindly.

Clara looked into his eyes and smiled. She was glad that Lawrence was amiable for the dinner, even though the two of them had barely spoken in months. "Thank you, Lawrence. Happy Thanksgiving."

Sam was in line behind Fiona at the buffet. "Fiona," he said quietly. "Is it alright if I sit next to you at dinner?"

Fiona was glad she was facing away from him so that he could not see how red her face had become. "Yes, of course," she said over her shoulder. She took her plate and waited for Sam to finish getting his. Then they found two seats together at the table and chose their places there.

When everyone had finished being seated, Clara tapped a fork against her wine glass. "Today we give thanks that we have survived the most difficult year that our country has known since the War of the Rebellion. Let us celebrate life and abundance and be thankful that we have made it this far! There is plenty of food, so don't be shy if you would like a second helping."

William laughed. "How about a third helping?"

Clara grinned. "You should not be shy about a third helping, Dr. Hamilton, especially since you have been away saving so many lives. We might not have a town anymore if not for you, and we are thankful to you for your efforts."

Sam turned to Fiona. "I'm thankful for you," he said. "You've been a great friend…helped me get through a bad time."

"I'm thankful you never had to go to War," Fiona replied shyly. "Thank goodness they never came for you." She felt her heart flutter when Sam took her hand under the table and held it gently. She was afraid to try to eat from her plate because she knew it would mean she had to let go of his hand. Instead she was content to watch the others, who were having a merry time.

Abigail did not touch the tray of dinner that was brought to her upstairs room. She watched through the window, trying her best to ignore the sinking feeling that this would be another holiday season without her husband.

The snow began to fall heavy. Fires crackled in every room, but it was difficult to keep up with the chill that was felt off every window. Abigail watched the snowflakes from her bed, growing more uncomfortable every day from the heaviness of her belly. Mary walked in to check on her. "I have to attend a birth now, even though I just returned from one," she giggled. "It is not too far, so I decided to take Dolly." She looked at Abigail's belly and shook her head. "I really think it will be any day now. Haven't you felt anything happening?"

"Not yet, Mary. You will be the first to know if I do,"

Abigail replied. "Is William coming for Christmas dinner tomorrow?"

"I'm afraid not. Apparently, this outbreak is worse than the one we had in the springtime. William is waiting for help from the Red Cross. None of us know how long it will be before they arrive in Yorktown."

Abigail smiled at Mary. "You mustn't worry, Mary. I have a feeling that the Red Cross will arrive just in time."

Mary spent more hours at the birth than she was expecting, and was not able to leave until the next morning. After she had finished attending the new mother, she packed her medical kit into one of her saddlebags, but began to feel dizzy and weak. "What's happening to me?" she whispered as she felt a sudden turning in her stomach. She climbed onto Dolly and nudged her with the sides of her boots. As Dolly trotted along, Mary could feel herself becoming ill. She pulled on the reigns and dismounted just in time to feel herself purging into the snow. She took deep breaths and tried to steady herself, but suddenly recalled that the house she had been to the previous day had a child who was ill. "Oh no," she said under her breath. She climbed back onto Dolly and made her way to the house as quickly as she could.

She dismounted shortly before reaching the stable. Sam came out to meet her. "Are you alright, Mrs. Hamilton?"

"Stay away, Sam. I'm not alright. I believe I have the influenza," she explained, her voice catching in her throat.

Sam backed away and waited for her to go into the house before he took Dolly to the stable. Mary went straight into the library and telephoned the clinic. "William, I'm sorry to bother you. The house I attended yesterday had a child who was ill. I have just remembered it, but now I am feeling dreadful. It hurts me to even move."

"Alright, Mary," William said, choking on his words. "Go to your bedroom and do not let anyone in the house come near you."

Mary felt tears rolling down her cheeks. "I'm sorry, William."

"There's nothing to be sorry about. Many have recovered from this illness, so do not give up hope. I will be there as soon as I can."

"I love you," she said tearfully.

"I love you, Mary. Goodbye."

Mary took each heavy step up the staircase, grasping the rail for support. When she made it to her bedroom, she found a red ribbon and tied it onto the doorknob to warn the staff. She then lay on her bed and blacked out.

Clara felt her heart sink when she saw the ribbon on Mary's door. "Mary," she called, knocking softly on the door. "Mary, are you alright?" When no answer came, she hurried downstairs to the servants' quarters and addressed the maids. "Mary has marked her door to show that she is suffering from influenza. No one is to enter her room under any circumstances. When you bring a tray for her, leave it just outside the door, but do not take it inside. Mr. Collins has telephoned to say that he will not be attending Christmas dinner after all, and with Abigail confined to her room...the dinner will be put on hold until further notice. I have given permission for Mrs. Malone to visit her family until the New Year, and I don't imagine we will require much cooking while the men are away and the ladies are confined to their rooms. Be sure to remember about Mary's illness—it is of utmost importance that it not be allowed to spread in this house."

The maids nodded worriedly. Clara returned up the stairs to a loud cry coming from Abigail's room. She hurried inside to find her wailing on the bed. "Is the baby coming?"

"No," Abigail sobbed. "Ethan cannot forgive me, and this anguish is my punishment. Or else he has died and that is why he will not return my letters. Either way, he is never coming back!"

"You must calm yourself, dear. If there was anything I could do for you—"

"Clara, will you go to him?" she pleaded. "Just be sure he is still alive. I'm afraid something has happened to him!"

"I will go to him," Clara said, trying to calm her down. "You just stay here and rest. Tell the maids if you need anything."

Abigail sighed in relief. "Thank you, Clara. You are a dear friend. Thank you for going to see him." Clara put on her coat, then she and Sam began the snowy drive to the ranch in Yorktown.

Ethan was grooming the horses in one of the buildings. He was stunned to see Clara walk inside. He felt as though his heart stopped. "Has something happened to Abigail?"

"So you *do* care for her," Clara said in a scolding tone. "Do you know how many days she has waited in agony for you to come home?"

"I can't go back, Clara." He took a deep breath and continued with a shaking voice, "I've decided to give Abigail a divorce."

Clara gasped. "Ethan, you wouldn't!" She was too shocked to say more.

Ethan looked away from her and explained quietly,

"People have come to expect divorce now. They blame the War. It's not as shameful as it once was…"

"If you are going to tell me it's because you don't love Abigail anymore, then I won't believe it. I saw how worried you were to see me when you thought something might have happened to her."

"Of course I love her, Clara. It is why I will give her the divorce. Then she can be free to be happy with someone else."

"You speak as if you are doing her a favor, when in truth she is heartbroken at home, believing you are staying away because you can't forgive her."

"That's not it at all," Ethan sighed. "I'm worried I will hurt her."

"Then how could you even suggest a divorce? She is Catholic anyway, she doesn't believe in it. If you tell her that you want a divorce now, it will not just hurt her. It will cripple her forever."

Ethan looked helplessly at Clara. "Then I don't know what to do."

"Come home to Abigail. She needs you desperately. If you could see how anguished she was when you did not come for Thanksgiving or return any of her letters…"

"I couldn't read them," Ethan confessed. "I knew that if I did, I would come rushing back to her—but I'm afraid of hurting her. The War messed up my mind, Clara. William had to stop me from hurting her one night. I didn't know what I was doing. William said we had to sleep separately or I might really harm her. Abigail deserves a chance with someone she doesn't have to be afraid of. I hoped that if I stayed away, it would be like I never came back, when she was better off without me."

"I didn't realize that was the reason you left," she replied sadly. "There must be a solution that is not divorce. What about the baby?"

Ethan looked mortified. "Abigail is pregnant?"

"You didn't know?" she cried impatiently. "She's due to have the baby at any minute!"

He clutched his chest in sorrow. "And you're sure she still wants me?"

"Yes!" Clara exclaimed. "It's why I'm here. Come home, even if it is only for an hour. She will feel better the instant she sees that you still care for her. If you are worried about sleeping near her in the house, you can move into the stable apartment with Sam."

Ethan looked at her mournfully. "Please, take me to her."

"There's something else you should know," Clara remembered emotionally. "Mary is not well. She has tied a red ribbon on her bedroom door."

Ethan's face crumpled. "Let's hurry." They climbed into the car with Sam and drove away from Yorktown.

At the house, Fiona was startled by Abigail loudly calling for her. "Fiona, help!" she cried.

Fiona rushed up the stairs to find Abigail leaning over the bed in pain. "Is the baby coming?"

"Yes! Has Mary returned? I need her to come now!"

Fiona ran to Mary's bedroom, but stopped suddenly when she saw the ribbon on the doorknob. She returned hastily to Abigail's side. "Miss Mary cannot come. Should I telephone Dr. Hamilton?"

"There isn't time for him to come," cried Abigail. "Go fetch Mrs. Malone."

"She has already left for the holiday. There is only me and the two maids!"

Abigail cried out in pain as she held onto the bed. "Then go get Phillip. He will help."

Fiona's eyes grew wide. "You want me to bring Mr. Valenti?"

"Yes, tell him to come now!" she urged, and cried out again.

Fiona ran to the farmhouse and breathlessly told Phillip that Abigail was having the baby. He stared at her in disbelief. "Are you sure she asked for me?"

"Yes, she insisted that you come. Clara and Mary cannot help her, and I don't know what to do!"

Phillip turned to tell Gabriella that he was leaving for a little while, then he hurried with Fiona back to the house. When he got to Abigail's bedroom, she was already on the bed, crying in pain, and beginning to push. "Bring linens, a pot of water, and a ball of twine," he told Fiona. She left the room to gather the items.

"I can feel it being born!" Abigail moaned.

Phillip rushed to her and caught the baby in his shaking hands. The cord was wound tight around the baby's neck and its face began to turn blue. When Fiona returned to the room, Phillip was unwrapping the cord and breathing into the baby's mouth.

"What's wrong?" Abigail pleaded. "Has my child lived?"

Phillip continued to breathe into the baby's mouth and Fiona watched in dismay. It seemed like hours, but it was only moments before the shrill cry of a newborn began echoing from the walls. Phillip placed the baby into Abigail's arms and attended to her until the cord could be tied off with the twine.

When Ethan entered the house, he heard the shrieking cry of the baby. He ran upstairs to Abigail's room, where Phillip and Fiona were there with her. The room went quiet. Ethan stared at Phillip in silence. The tension was felt by all, since neither Ethan nor Phillip expected to see the other at that moment. When Fiona spoke to Ethan, it jolted them back into reality. "I begged him to come help. The baby wouldn't breathe and Mr. Valenti saved his life."

It seemed as if everyone held their breath as they waited for what might happen next. Ethan finally stepped toward Phillip and slowly extended his hand. Neither of them said a word as they shook hands, the same as they did in the War, before everything changed for everyone. After shaking hands, Phillip quietly left the room and Ethan turned to Abigail.

"You're here," she said breathlessly, but her face radiating with joy. "You came back to me."

Ethan kneeled beside the bed and leaned forward to kiss her. "I'm sorry I stayed away. I should have written you back. I never meant to worry you or make you think I didn't care. The truth is, I love you with all my heart and only thought I was doing what's best for us."

Abigail took his hand. "Thank you for coming home," she whispered. She weakly held the baby out for him to hold.

When Ethan took the baby into his arms, he gazed at the small face with wonder, and spoke quietly. "He is perfect, Abigail. He has not seen war or the terrible things in life. I'll do anything to ensure he never has to." Abigail felt tears filling her eyes as she observed how gently he held the baby, and how proud he was to gaze upon the sleeping child in his arms.

At the farmhouse, Phillip was slumped over the kitchen table, holding his heads in his hands. He looked up suddenly when he heard the front door creak open. Serena stood alone in the open doorway. "Brother!" she exclaimed. She rushed to put her arms around him and kiss his tear-stained face. "How good to see you! Are the children alright?"

Phillip nodded and wiped his eyes. "The children are sleeping."

"What's wrong?" she asked in concern. "You've been crying."

Phillip shook his head dismissively. "How was your visit with Angelina?"

Serena lowered her head. "I never saw her, and no one knows where she is. The whole family she lived with was taken by influenza, but Angelina was not found among the dead. I've searched, but I've run out of money and had no choice but to come back without her."

"You can have what money I have left," Phillip offered.

Serena looked hopeful. "Do you have one hundred dollars?"

Phillip groaned. "I probably have twenty. What do you need one hundred dollars for?"

"There's an investigator for hire in Pittsburgh. The folks in town say he can find anyone. That's why his fee is so high."

"We'll figure out something." Phillip stood up and headed for his bedroom. Without turning to look at Serena, he said emotionally, "How did you do it? How did you walk away from your child, knowing you could never raise her yourself like it ought to be?"

Serena thought about it and answered in a low voice. "The only way I could bear it was knowing she was raised in a better life than I could give her. Even so…it has been dreadful for me to be without her. Now I fear I have lost her forever." She could hear Phillip begin to cry from where he stood. "Brother, what happened when I was away?" But Phillip kept walking to his bedroom and closed the door behind him.

At the same time in Davenport House, Ethan left Abigail's bedroom to find Clara, who was waiting in the hallway. "You were right," he told her. "Thank you for coming to talk some sense into me."

"I was glad to. You will be so busy with the new baby that you'll forget you ever considered those things. Now, there is something for Abigail under the Christmas tree. Could you bring it up? You'll know it when you see it," she grinned.

Ethan went downstairs to the Christmas tree while Clara entered the bedroom to see the baby.

"Oh, he is just perfect," Clara whispered as she held him in her arms. "Do you have a name for him yet?"

"I think so. I have to see if Ethan agrees to it first," Abigail blushed.

Clara nodded confidently. "He will agree to anything you say, so long as it makes you happy." She contentedly held and rocked the sleeping baby in her arms.

Just down the hallway, Mary awoke in her dark room to a warm hand being placed to her forehead. She looked up disoriented. "William? Are you really here?"

He stood over her in concern. "I'm here," he said, his voice cracking with emotion. "The Red Cross has arrived at the clinic. I'm going to stay with you now."

"I'm sorry about all this," Mary said, beginning to weep. "I did everything I could to save the Randall baby yesterday. But the whole family might be gone by now."

"I saw the Randalls in town. They and the baby looked fine," William explained.

Mary put her hand to her heart. "Oh, thank God."

"When did the fever start?" William asked, stroking her hair.

"Well, I suppose I've not had a fever yet. But I hurt all over, and I am ill at the thought of eating."

William abruptly switched on the lamp on the bedside table. Mary squinted from the light and groaned. "I must look terrible just now. I've had no time to fix myself up while I've been ill."

William studied her face and a smile slowly crossed his lips. "On the contrary, you look better than ever." He reached out to stroke her cheek. "I don't think you had influenza at all."

Mary sat up in bed. "What do you mean? I felt dreadful all morning!"

William laughed heartily and kissed her face. "You'll find out soon enough."

Mary gasped. "Do you really think—? Oh, I'm so embarrassed!" She covered her face with her hands and started crying again. "I don't even know why I'm crying."

William handed her a handkerchief. "I do. And I couldn't be happier."

Mary uncovered her face. "Then, I can go see Abigail and the baby!"

"Yes, you can," William smiled. "But don't leave just yet. I worried for you all day and now that I know you are alright, I just want to feel you next to me again." He lay down beside her and draped his arm around her waist.

Mary relaxed next to him. "Oh, I almost forgot to tell you—" she began, but William had already fallen asleep.

Mary watched him for a moment and kissed his forehead. "Merry Christmas, William."

Mary decided she could not wait a minute longer to see the baby and she quietly slipped out of the room. When she looked into Abigail's bedroom, she found Clara proudly holding a bundle in her arms.

"I can't believe I missed it!" groaned Mary.

"Mary," Abigail smiled to see her. "Clara said you might have been ill. You must be feeling better."

Mary sat next to Abigail on the bed and shook her head. "I'm embarrassed now. It was not influenza at all. Now I'm just sorry I missed the birth."

Abigail took her hand. "I am glad you are here now."

Clara gently handed Mary the baby. "Isn't he just brilliant?"

"He is," Mary agreed, tears streaming down her cheeks.

"Mary, you're glowing," Abigail remarked, giving Mary a knowing look.

"What is his name?" asked Mary.

"I'm waiting to speak with Ethan," Abigail replied, just as Ethan came through the doorway with a heavy object. Abigail gasped when she saw what he carried with him. He carefully set it on the floor beside the bed.

"Merry Christmas, Abigail," Clara told her.

Abigail gazed lovingly at the intricately carved wooden cradle that was wrapped in a big red bow. She turned to Clara. "It's beautiful. Thank you, Clara."

Ethan walked around the bed to hold her hand. "Do you have a name for our son?"

Abigail looked bashful. "I'd like to name him Patrick, for the saint of Ireland. Only if you agree, of course."

"It is a good name," he replied, taking the baby to hold in his arms. "Should we see if he likes his new bed?"

Abigail nodded happily. Ethan laid the baby on the soft mattress and whispered to him, "Merry Christmas, Patrick, my perfect son."

Clara and Mary left the room quietly. "I'm glad to see you well, Mary," Clara told her.

Mary blushed. "Thank you. It turned out to be a lovelier Christmas than I ever could have imagined."

Clara laughed. "And you have not even opened my gift to you! And the dinner has been put on hold. Come, let us go down to the Christmas tree and ensure everyone receives their presents and gets their dinner."

In the servants' quarters of the house, Fiona quietly slipped through the kitchen and exited the door to the outside. She went to the stable and knocked on the door of Sam's apartment. He smiled when he opened the door. "Hello, Fiona."

"I have something wonderful to tell you. You are now the uncle of a fine baby boy," she announced proudly.

Sam's face broke out into a smile. "She had the baby?"

Fiona nodded and giggled in delight. "He is lovely. I am certain Miss Abigail would like you to see the new little one, but Mr. Ethan is in there with her now."

"Abby will be happy now that he is here."

"Yes, I believe she will be," Fiona replied. Then she became nervous. "I have something for you—it's a present."

"That was nice of you," he said. Fiona brought her hand around from behind her back and held a set of matching knit gloves, scarf, and hat. Sam grinned. "Did you make these?"

"I did, in my spare time," she answered shyly.

"Thank you. You didn't have to do that."

"I wanted to. Merry Christmas, Sam." Fiona smiled at him and turned to leave.

"Wait," he said. "I hoped I could get your opinion on something." He quickly went into the apartment and returned with a small box. "Do you think Abby might like these?" he asked nervously. "I never know what to get for a girl's present."

Fiona admired the silver hair combs with butterfly engraving. "They are lovely, Sam. I'm sure she will like them."

"Oh," he smiled sheepishly. "In that case, I have something to confess. I really got these for you, but I didn't know if you would like them."

Fiona looked up hopefully. "Did you truly?"

Sam nodded and laughed. "I already gave Abby her present this morning."

Fiona laughed too. "Thank you for this beautiful gift," she told him. "I've never had something nice like this before."

He smiled proudly. "I'm glad I chose right, then. You've been a real help to me this year, and I want you to have a Merry Christmas and Happy New Year."

"Thank you, Sam," she blushed. "But does this mean you will have to save for longer to buy the land from Miss Clara?"

He looked at her admiringly. "I don't mind, Fiona. I can be patient. Some things in life are worth the wait."

DAVENPORT HOUSE

House Secrets

MARIE SILK

"Abby…Abby, wake up." Sam gently shook her awake.

"Sam? What are you doing here?" she asked sleepily. Abigail sat up in bed and immediately checked on the baby, who was sleeping peacefully beside her. She shielded the baby's eyes while she switched on the bedside lamp. "What time is it?"

Sam did not answer. He looked at her with fear in his eyes. "I found Mr. Collins."

"Had he gone missing?" she questioned. "I did not realize. Where is he now?"

"In the field behind the stable. I tried to rouse him, but—he's dead, Abby."

Abigail drew a sharp breath. "Was Ethan with you?"

"No, he slept in his room the whole night. I didn't know what to do when I found Mr. Collins like that, so I came here to wake you. You know everyone in this house better than me. What do I do?"

"We must wake Clara and tell her there has been an accident. Mr. Collins will need to be carried inside so he may be laid out in the parlor. We will see to the burial when Clara is ready."

"Abby," Sam shook his head, lowering his voice to a whisper. "I don't think it was an accident."

…coming Winter of 2016…

About the Author

Marie Silk has enjoyed writing stories in many genres since childhood. She lives with her family in the United States and frequently travels the globe to learn more about the world and the people in it. Marie is inspired by history and the feats of humanity from ancient civilization to present day. She is the author of the Davenport House family saga.

For contact details and information on upcoming releases, please visit: MarieSilk.com.